Two Dead in Three Seconds

The Texas town of El Paso was in the grip of anarchy and corruption when Dallas Stoudenmire rode into town. Fearless as any outlaw and quicker on the draw than most, he is appointed city marshal and sets about cleaning up the town.

But the Manning brothers think they own El Paso and they have the boss of the local Texas Rangers in their pocket. They will resort to any means to run Stoudenmire out of town and there aren't many who will stand in their way.

But Stoudenmire enlists the support of the city's most notorious Mexican, and these two men make a formidable team. The bloodbath that ensues leaves no one in any doubt as to who really runs El Paso.

By the same author

Top Gun For Hire
Casper's Courage
Trouble at Gila Bend
Kentucky Killer

Two Dead in Three Seconds

DEREK TAYLOR

A Black Horse Western

ROBERT HALE · LONDON

© Derek Taylor 2001
First published in Great Britain 2001

ISBN 0 7090 6891 3

Robert Hale Limited
Clerkenwell House
Clerkenwell Green
London EC1R 0HT

The right of Derek Taylor to be identified as
author of this work has been asserted by him
in accordance with the Copyright, Designs and
Patents Act 1988.

SANDWELL LIBRARY & INFORMATION SERVICE	
I1680088	
Cypher	13.8.01
W	£10.50

Typeset by
Derek Doyle & Associates, Liverpool.
Printed and bound in Great Britain by
Antony Rowe Limited, Wiltshire

For Ron Moore

Two Dead in Three Seconds

ONE

Dallas Stoudenmire looked down Main Street and fingered the badge he'd just pinned to his chest. He smirked to himself, knowing what it was going to cost the greedy city fathers of El Paso. They were used to paying their lawmen a percentage of fines levied for arrests but Stoudenmire had told them what they could do with it and they ended up paying him twice what any marshal had ever been paid in El Paso plus the percentage of fines levied. The city was rowdy and turbulent and he knew he would not be leaving it a poor man.

'What's on the menu, Doc?' he asked, stepping into the Globe Restaurant on El Paso Street.

'Doc' was Samuel M. Cummings, the man he'd ridden into El Paso with. He was not a medical doctor but for years, ever since he'd saved a man's life in the Civil War by cutting off his badly wounded arm, everyone had called him 'Doc'.

'Why, you old son of a gun!' Doc Cummings exclaimed on catching sight of the badge on Stoudenmire's chest.

'Marshal Son Of a Gun,' Stoudenmire corrected him.

'Whatever,' Cummings laughed. 'I suppose you could say: now we've arrived.'

'Yeah. You feed 'em and I'll hang 'em and we'll both have something to fall back on when we're old and grey,' remarked Stoudenmire, six foot two in height and handsome enough to cut a dash.

'Who says we're gonna make old bones?'

'The bullet has not been moulded that could kill me.'

Doc said nothing in reply. From anyone else, such brave talk might have caused him to shake his head in disbelief at the arrogance of man. But when the words came from his brother-in-law, Dallas Stoudenmire, who'd ridden through more storms of lead than the devil himself and survived, he accepted there could be some truth to them.

'Well,' he said, indicating to Stoudenmire that

Two Dead in Three Seconds

he should take a seat, 'perhaps the egg has been laid that can nourish you.'

Stoudenmire laughed and sat down at the nearest table. While he was tucking into the kind of meal he liked, a party of Mexican *vaqueros* rode into town. Making the kind of showing that everyone noticed, they reined in their horses outside the Globe Restaurant and dismounted. Before long they were met by fellow countrymen living in El Paso and a verbal commotion ensued.

'What do you suppose all that din is about?' Stoudenmire asked Doc, who was sitting down at a table with him sipping from a cup of coffee.

'Search me,' replied Doc.

'Well, perhaps I'd better step out and see,' Stoudenmire said, dabbing his mouth with a linen napkin. 'Sounds to me like it's getting a bit heated out there.'

Doc Cummings gave him a look that told him to be careful. Getting up from the table Stoudenmire, who didn't wear holsters but preferred to carry a gun in each of two leather-lined hip pockets, didn't answer him. Instead he made sure his guns, one of which was a sawn-off barrel-belly gun, were safely in place. Cummings was not in the habit of following on his brother-

Two Dead in Three Seconds

in-law's heels when he was law-keeping and he didn't do so this time. Instead he poured himself another cup of coffee while keeping an eye peeled on Stoudenmire as he stepped out of the restaurant door on to the boardwalk outside. There were about twelve *vaqueros* all seemingly talking at once. When they saw the shiny badge on Stoudenmire's chest and realized who he was they all fell silent. Stoudenmire, standing tall at all of his six feet two inches, eyeballed the man he took to be their leader.

'What happened to Campbell?' the man suddenly asked.

'Campbell? Who the hell is Campbell?' Stoudenmire replied, slipping a hand into each of his pockets.

'He was the marshal of this city,' the Mexican answered.

'Well, as you can see, he ain't no more.'

'No,' remarked the Mexican, walking up to the boardwalk and putting a foot on the steps leading up to the Globe Restaurant. 'Well then, maybe you can tell me what has happened to my men. They were looking for rustled cattle but they ain't been seen by nobody about these parts for a week or more.'

Two Dead in Three Seconds

'They been killed, I told you, out at the Hale Ranch,' said another Mexican. 'Campbell and John Hale did it. We're wasting our time here, let's go get them.'

'Hold it now,' Stoudenmire said. 'If there's any arresting to do round here, I'll do it.'

As he spoke he pointed a thumb at his marshal's badge.

'Ain't no gringo ever arrested another gringo for killing a Mexican,' the leader of the *vaqueros* declared.

'If there's any truth in what you're claiming, this gringo will arrest Campbell and John Hale, but if you go taking the law into your own hands you're likely to get into a lot of trouble,' Stoudenmire warned him.

The Mexican eyeballed Stoudenmire for a second or two, but then decided there was no more to be said on the matter. Suddenly he turned and walked to his horse and pulled the reins from the hitching rail to which he'd tied them.

'We'll see, gringo,' was all he said by way of reply as he swung up on to his horse's saddle. Then, as his men followed suit, he got his horse under control and rode at a gallop out of El Paso.

Two Dead in Three Seconds

Stoudenmire watched them go. He in turn was studied by the small gathering of El Paso Mexicans left behind. Despite their fear and loathing of white men in general, they all to a man reckoned him the kind of lawman they could depend upon. That, though, could only mean one thing. Hard times in El Paso for those who liked to think the town was their own.

Suddenly there was the sound of gunfire. It was obvious that a commotion had broken out in the saloon across the road from Doc Cummings's restaurant. Stoudenmire turned his gaze in the saloon's direction just in time to see a man come flying out and land in the dust clutching a wound in his stomach from which blood was gushing. He was quickly followed by another man. He had a Colt Frontier in each hand and was patently set to finish off his man.

'Drop 'em!' Stoudenmire yelled, as the Mexicans ran for cover.

The man squinted into the bright sunlight of the day to try and get a picture of who was giving him orders. Last time he was in town the city marshal was Campbell, a man everyone who crossed him soon discovered to be pretty inadequate. Assuming the figure standing before him now was still that same city marshal, the man, a dirty, drunken cowpoke whom no cattle rancher would waste his time employing, lifted his guns to gesticulate derisively at Stoudenmire. It was as far as he got. Quicker than a bolt of lightning, Stoudenmire drew from his right pocket a Smith & Wesson Pocket .32 and fired it. It sent the cowpoke back into the saloon quicker than he came out.

The lowlife lying on the ground clutching his belly tried to look around to see who it was that had come to his rescue. It was surely not Campbell. He craned his neck in time to see Stoudenmire stepping towards him.

'Thank'ee, sir,' he said, pressing a hand down hard on his stomach in a vain attempt to stop the pain and blood.

Stoudenmire did not wait to acknowledge the man's gratitude but instead started to walk towards the entrance to the saloon. His impulse was to put him out of his misery but further thought told him he'd be dead in a few minutes anyway from loss of blood, so why waste a bullet? He'd hardly gone three steps past him, when the batwings of the saloon were thrown open to reveal another cowpoke coming through. On seeing that Stoudenmire was not who he expected him to be, the man exclaimed, 'You ain't Campbell!'

'No,' replied Stoudenmire, 'that I ain't.'

He kept on walking up the steps to the boardwalk and past the cowpoke into the saloon. Lying dead on the floor near the bar was the cowboy Stoudenmire had shot. Walking up to him, stopping and pointing a finger down at the corpse, Stoudenmire warned the quietened drinkers that things had changed in El Paso City. Given what they had just witnessed, no one doubted it. Though one man did question it. Not out loud, but to himself. His name was George Manning, the saloon's owner. He was one of three brothers who'd long since come to think of downtown El Paso as being their own. Whatever ideas to the contrary the city council might have.

TWO

'You reckon the bodies of those two *vaqueros* are still lying out there amongst the sage?' George Campbell, ex-city marshal of El Paso asked John Hale.

They were sitting in Hale's ranch house in Canutillo, some twelve miles upstream from El Paso.

'Reckon so,' Hale replied. 'Ain't nothing but wild animals and vermin out there.'

'Ain't been but a few days. You think they'll still be recognizable?'

'Most likely, though I don't think you'd be able to tell the colour of their eyes, or even if they started out with any.' Hale smirked. He hated Mexicans and always took a grim delight in watching any one of them bite the dust for whatever reason.

'Well, you know those *vaqueros* your son said are out there looking for them are gonna find them, don't you, John?'

Campbell was a half-decent man who was easily led by friend and foe alike. After being fired as the marshal of El Paso for failing to arrest trouble makers in sufficient numbers to make an impact on the lawlessness of the fast-growing city, he'd decided to hang out at his friend Hale's ranch. He knew Hale was rustling Mexican cattle but had been persuaded to turn a blind eye to the fact; not for financial gain but because he'd been persuaded it was a customary thing to do in these parts. He knew too, though he wasn't happy about it, that Mexicans died in trying to shield their cattle from the American rustlers and he wasn't altogether comfortable with it.

'So? What can they prove? Besides, there ain't no one in El Paso gonna do anything about it.'

Just at that moment Hale's eldest son, Josh, came riding into the home place.

'They found them, Pa,' he called out to Hale as he dismounted and tied his horse to a hitching rail in front of the house, the veranda of which Hale and Campbell were sitting on. 'And they's

Two Dead in Three Seconds

kicking up a mighty stink, saying they know you stole their cattle and killed the Mexicans. I heard too, Pa, there's a new marshal in town who's promised them the law will see whoever killed them pays the price.'

'New marshal in town? You know anything about that?' Hale asked Campbell.

'How should I know?' Campbell replied. 'I been here with you since they fired me.'

'Well, best we go into town and see.'

Hale knew he had nothing to fear from the law anywhere in the vicinity of the Rio Grande. The leader of the *vaqueros* had been right when he'd told Stoudenmire there hadn't ever been a gringo who'd arrested another gringo for killing a Mexican. And, besides which, he himself hadn't pulled the trigger that killed the *vaqueros*, and who could prove any of his cowboys had?

'All right,' agreed Campbell. 'I'd be interested to see who the dang fool is that has stepped into my shoes.'

They arrived hot on the heels of the *vaqueros* who'd brought the dead bodies of their *compadres* into town. They'd gone straight to Stoudenmire's office. A mob of El Paso Mexicans had quickly gathered around the *vaqueros*.

Two Dead in Three Seconds

'Marshal,' the leader of the *vaqueros* said to Stoudenmire. 'You wanted proof. Now you have it. These are the bodies of my two men. We found them dead under a tree on Hale's land. They were shot in cold blood while sitting have a smoke. The cigarillos were still in their hands.'

'All right, all right, now let me see them,' Stoudenmire said, pushing his way through the throng of people.

The two dead men had been brought to town in the back of a buckboard with a poncho thrown over each of their faces. Stoudenmire pulled back the ponchos and looked at each man in turn. He was just throwing back the ponchos when George Campbell and John Hale rode into El Paso Street. The mob turned on them instantly and started accusing them of murdering the two men. Sensing that things could turn pretty nasty in a very short time, Stoudenmire was quick to act.

'This ain't the place to hold a trial,' he declared forcefully.

'We didn't shoot nobody,' John Hale insisted, repeating the claim he'd been making since coming up against the mob.

Campbell had been saying nothing, just keep-

Two Dead in Three Seconds

ing his horse tightly reined in and his eyes fixed firmly on those of the Mexicans who looked like they could at any moment pull him and Hale from their horses and carry out a lynching.

'My men died on your ranch, Hale, and that's enough proof for me. We already know you been stealing our cattle for months now,' insisted the leader of the *vaqueros*. 'I say we should hang 'em now.'

'Not without a trial,' Stoudenmire pronounced in equally insistent tones.

'You gotta have an inquest first,' Campbell interrupted, 'to find out how the men died.'

The eyes of the mob became fixed on Campbell. It was obvious they held him in some contempt. Stoudenmire was interested to see it, since here was the man the citizens of El Paso had denigrated for being so ineffectual as city marshal. Still, nobody had said he was corrupt which, in any genuine lawman's opinion, was the worst thing that could be said against anyone who wore the badge.

'The man's right,' Stoudenmire told the mob. 'I'll see the judge and get one convened before the day is out. Y'all will be told the place and time.'

Stoudenmire was the sort of man who instilled

Two Dead in Three Seconds

confidence in people and the leader of the *vaqueros* decided to trust him.

'OK,' he declared. 'But you pull a fast one, Marshal, and we'll kill every gringo who crosses our path. And you two will be first,' he snarled, turning to face Campbell and Hale. Looking back at him defiantly, Hale slowly turned his horse away from the mob and pointed it in the direction of a hitching rail outside a saloon once called the Ben Dowell Saloon but which had recently been renamed the Manning Saloon. It was the same saloon in which Stoudenmire had announced in so peremptory a manner to the low life of El Paso that he was the new marshal. Its owner, George Manning, was standing just inside looking over the batwings. Hale caught his eye and knew that the look in it was an invitation to him and Campbell to come in and seek common cause. Stoudenmire offered some extra reassurance to the Mexicans and then turned and walked away. Manning watched him go.

Since arriving in El Paso Stoudenmire had made the acquaintance of one of the city's most notorious citizens. Her name was Belle Starr. She'd come to the city a few months back and taken over one of its most infamous establish-

Two Dead in Three Seconds

ments, the Silver Dollar Hotel. She'd kept on the good-time girls who plied their trade there, but had added a touch of glamour to the place, making it all the more attractive to the men of the city who desired to buy favours from pretty girls. George Manning reckoned Belle Starr to be his girl and had resented Stoudenmire striking up an acquaintance with her. Guessing where he was going, Manning became riled and muttered to himself, 'Son of a gun! You'd better just go and sell your wares some place else.'

He might have gone striding over to show Stoudenmire that someone else had already staked a claim to the affections of Belle Starr, were it not for the fact that Campbell and Hale suddenly appeared, pushing their way through the batwings into the saloon.

'What d'you make of him?' Hale asked as he approached the bar.

The barkeep, who knew Hale as a regular, was already pouring him a shot of redeye.

'I don't,' Manning replied. 'I don't wanna make anything of him at all.'

'Well, looks to me like you better, Manning, 'cause things ain't gonna be the same round here no more, if he stays as marshal.'

'That's a big if,' Manning replied. 'We've seen off more than a dozen city marshals since we've been here. If you'd kept your job, Campbell, we wouldn't have a new marshal to have to deal with.'

'That ain't my fault. If you'd kept your men under some sort of control I'd still have my job. If folks are shooting up the town the law's supposed to arrest 'em. I told you they'd get someone else to do it if I didn't.'

'Yeah, well, you didn't have to get drunker than all of them put together. That was just plumb stupid and is what's landed us up in this trouble.'

'We'll just have to sort it, then, won't we?' Hale declared, taking his shot-glass from the counter and knocking it back. It was filled again by the barkeep almost before he'd slapped it back down on the counter. Screwing up his face to help his palate absorb the first shot of redeye, he assaulted his taste-buds with the next.

'How we gonna do that?' Campbell asked, picking up a glass of beer the barkeep had poured for him and sipping from it.

'We'll wait until after the inquest and then we'll get him,' Manning declared. 'No point in trying anything until then, with the whole town's eyes upon him.'

Two Dead in Three Seconds

'Funny he don't seem to carry a weapon,' Campbell remarked.

'He carries one all right,' Manning sneered. 'Only in his pockets and not in a holster. He's fast, too. Saw it with my own eyes.'

Just then one of Manning's brothers, Felix, joined them. He'd seen from the Coliseum, the saloon he ran, what had gone on and had come to discuss with his brother what was to be done.

While they talked Stoudenmire was getting better acquainted with Miss Starr, who invited him to dine with her later that evening after the inquest was over. She'd given an invitation to dine that night to George Manning the day before, but she reckoned it'd be easy enough to send word to him that she had a headache. A bigshot in town was one thing, but a tall, dark, handsome marshal who could carry himself fearlessly was quite another.

THREE

Stoudenmire arranged for the inquest to take place at five o'clock in El Paso's newly built courthouse. The constable was former Texas Ranger Gus Krempau. He spoke Spanish well and was appointed to translate for the Mexicans. Judge Hooker presided and was soon calling for order in the proceedings, which were quickly turning into bedlam.

'Order! Order!' he shouted after an outburst from the Mexican who led the *vaqueros*. Once relative quiet had been achieved, he turned to the constable, saying, 'Mr Krempau, will you please tell me what was said.'

'He says, your honour, that he and his men found the bodies of their two comrades on ranch land belonging to Hale and that it was obvious they had been murdered by Campbell and Hale.'

As Krempau concluded his translation, the courthouse again erupted into chaos. While the Mexicans demanded justice, some of the American citizens of El Paso who had gathered in the courthouse taunted them with cries of 'prove it!'

'Ask them,' Judge Hooker called over the din, 'if they have any witnesses who will swear that Hale and Campbell murdered the two men.'

'Everyone knows they did it,' the leader of the *vaqueros* interrupted, throwing his hands up in the air and waving them forcefully at the bench. 'They been stealing our cattle for years.'

Again, the court erupted into bedlam with Mexicans on the one hand and Americans on the other, all shouting at each other. Judge Hooker was a fair man, but it was obvious to him that there was nothing except circumstantial evidence to implicate Campbell and Hale. After banging his gavel and calling for order but not achieving it, he pronounced over the deafening clatter of the din a verdict of unlawful death committed by persons unknown. Then he got up and retired from the bench, leaving Krempau to try and bring the proceedings to an end.

Krempau was someone in whom the Mexican

Two Dead in Three Seconds

residents of El Paso had in the past invested their trust. He spoke their language fluently and had lived and worked amongst them in various capacities for years.

'There will be an investigation into how your friends came to die,' he tried to reassure them. 'Our new city marshal has already told you that. If Campbell and Hale are found to be implicated in this terrible crime they will be brought to trial.'

Looking for support from Stoudenmire, who had been standing at the back of the court, Krempau saw that he had already left. He realized that only Stoudenmire could give the reassurance that might calm down the El Paso Mexicans and the *vaqueros*. He decided to try and catch up with him. He got to the door of the courthouse in time to see Stoudenmire disappearing into the Globe Restaurant half a block away.

'Whose side you on, anyway, constable?' Hale called out to Krempau as he stepped off the boardwalk to cross El Paso Street.

Hale, who had been drinking most of the afternoon in Manning's Saloon, was still nursing a bottle half-full of whiskey. Krempau at first ignored him, his eyes momentarily following a

Two Dead in Three Seconds

group of *vaqueros* carrying their dead comrades to Mexico, which began at the south end of El Paso Street. But Hale called out again, this time accusing him of trying, in his courtroom translations, to implicate him and Campbell.

'I translated the words of the Mexicans just as they spoke them,' he replied, stopping in the middle of the street and turning to face Campbell and Hale.

Campbell could hold his drink better than Hale and he wasn't anyway the sort of man who went spoiling for a fight. He said nothing but simply shrugged his shoulders angrily and threw Krempau a look of disgust. His horse wasn't tethered far away and he decided to go get it and book into a hotel.

'I'll take care of this, Campbell,' Hale called out, standing up straight and throwing his bottle aside. 'No one's gonna get away with trying to blame us for the death of dirty Mexicans.'

Before Krempau realized what was happening Hale pulled a gun and was able to make a lucky shot hit home. The shot knocked Krempau off his feet but as he hit the dirt he was able to pull his own gun and fire back at Hale. His shot though, was not so lucky and went wide of its mark.

Two Dead in Three Seconds

'You're a dirty dog, Constable, and now you're gonna die like one,' Hale spat at him, staggering over to where he'd fallen and standing over him ready to fire another shot.

'John!' Campbell, stunned by the cold bloodedness of what he was witnessing, called out to him, 'this ain't gonna help any.'

But before Hale could make any kind of reply, his head was suddenly thrown sideways and he was knocked off his feet. A bullet had thumped into his left temple, killing him instantly. Looking to see where it had come from, Campbell saw Stoudenmire stepping off the boardwalk outside the Globe Restaurant and coming towards him.

'This ain't my fight,' Campbell called out to Stoudenmire, letting go the reins of his horse and holding his hands out imploringly in front of him. Without altering his step any, Stoudenmire raised his gun, cocked it and let go a shot that hit Campbell in the heart. Most of the people who had been in the court were dispersing in various directions when the shoot-out had started. Stopped dead in their tracks by the sound of gunfire, they all looked on in utter disbelief at what had happened. A silence had fallen over El Paso Street but it did not last for long. It was broken by joyous exclamations coming from the Mexico end of the street.

'Marshal,' the leader of the *vaqueros* called out, taking a few steps back into Texas and America, 'we like you! We really like you! You come this side of town tonight and we buy you a drink. We give you a beautiful woman, too.'

'Is that so?' Stoudenmire muttered to himself, as he bent down to help Krempau to his feet. 'You hurt bad?' he asked him.

'No,' Krempau replied, 'thanks to you.'

'Good,' Stoudenmire remarked, adding as the constable balanced himself in a standing-up position. 'I guess you could say that solves the problem of who killed the *vaqueros*.'

Two men who might not have agreed with him were standing outside of Manning's Saloon, their eyes fixed firmly on Stoudenmire.

'He started it,' George Manning said to his brother Felix. 'Guess we're gonna have to finish it.'

'Yeah,' his brother agreed, 'and the sooner the better.'

As if he was psychic and had tuned into their thoughts, Stoudenmire turned and looked at the two brothers. Up to now he had known nothing of their ill-feeling towards him, nor of their evil machinations regarding his appointment as city marshal, but in the moment their eyes met across El Paso Street he realized the situation fully. He let his eyes remain fixed on theirs for long enough to make the brothers feel sufficiently uneasy to turn and retreat into their saloon.

Stoudenmire's attention was brought back to the matter of the shoot out by the sudden appearance of one of the city's undertakers.

'Take 'em away, Marshal?' the man asked Stoudenmire.

'Yeah,' Stoudenmire replied absent-mindedly, his thoughts having suddenly shifted on to the planned dinner he was to have that evening with Belle Starr.

Without taking his eyes off the Mannings' Saloon, he began to walk in the direction of his office. He decided he'd ask Belle that evening what she knew about the place and the people who owned it.

FOUR

'You do not own me, George Manning, and I will dine with whomsoever I choose to dine.'

George Manning had been drunk on not just the beauty of Belle Starr but also her feistiness ever since he and his brothers had ridden into El Paso some twelve months ago. It was true he'd always felt that she never did any more than play with his emotions, but that hadn't altered one bit how he felt towards her. Jealousy now was eating his heart out.

'But you don't even know Dallas Stoudenmire and you saw what he did yesterday. Why, he killed Campbell in cold blood, when anyone could see he was putting his hands up,' he remonstrated with her.

'George was a lily-livered waste of space who

got what was coming to him. The West is being tamed. You're either for the law or against it. Campbell couldn't make up his mind which.'

'I ain't ever heard you say you was for the law before now, Belle.'

'Well, I told you, George, things is changing. I got a good business and I don't aim to watch it shrivel and die because people's too afraid to come and settle in El Paso. If this town don't grow it's gonna die or get swamped by Mexicans.'

Manning couldn't believe that he was hearing such talk coming from the likes of Belle Starr. She was nothing more than the madame of a whorehouse and here she was talking as if she were one of the city righteous.

'What's come over you, Belle? You know that if this city gets any more respectable than it already is you'll be one of the first to be ran out of town.'

'I can accept change, George,' Belle replied, looking, to him, as lovely as ever in a beautifully cut silk dress, her hair perfectly coiffured in the fashion of the day. She still bore some of the scars of her frontier life. It was still obvious that buckskins would have hung as well on her as the fine dress she was wearing, but it was also obvious that she'd decided to play a new role in the life of the West and was more than capable of living up to it.

'And you think that the likes of Stoudenmire are part of that change?' Manning asked her, his voice full of bitterness.

'Well, you saw what happened last evening. John Hale was sowing the seeds of a border war between gringos and Mexicans that would have been fought out in and around the city. Dallas stopped it and I hear the city council are planning to make him a presentation in a show of gratitude. I think that means he's gonna be ringing the changes around here some for a while, don't you, George?'

Manning didn't care about what changes Stoudenmire was bringing about in El Paso, only that he was stealing the affections of someone he considered to be his girl. He was wrong about thinking that Belle was or ever could be his girl, but that didn't alter things. Dallas Stoudenmire was poking his nose into places no one, least of all he and his brothers, wanted him to and he was already planning his downfall.

'Well, we'll see about that, Belle,' he replied. 'And you'll soon find out he ain't no friend of yours. The city council has plans for El Paso Street that don't include you or the Silver Dollar and when Stoudenmire gets ordered by them to clean it up you'll see where your best interests lie.'

In response to what Manning was saying Belle could only bring to mind a picture of the night before when she lay making love in the arms of Stoudenmire. Later they had talked about their hopes and plans for the future and she had told him how she had plans to see her little whorehouse turn into the smartest hotel in El Paso. Just like the kind that they had back East. Stoudenmire had talked about settling down in El Paso and of maybe even going into politics. When he talked like that he was strong and masterful. She liked that in a man.

Manning sensed that she was enjoying some kind of reverie and could guess what it was all about. He'd been told that Stoudenmire had stepped into the Silver Dollar the evening before and had not stepped out again until early morning.

'Belle, didn't you hear what I just said?' he asked her, wanting to grip her by the shoulders and make her look into his eyes. He knew he

Two Dead in Three Seconds

didn't dare do such a thing though, not to a woman as headstrong as Belle Starr.

'I'm sorry, George,' Belle replied, snapping herself out of her day-dream, 'What were you—'

'I was saying . . .' he began to say but then decided he was wasting his time. 'Oh, never mind, Belle, you'll learn soon enough.'

With that he turned and without properly taking his leave of her walked out of the Silver Dollar Hotel. He'd realized that he and his brothers were going to have to deal with Stoudenmire in their own way.

A few blocks away in the city council chambers the mayor of El Paso was showing the appreciation of the citizens of the city for the start Marshal Stoudenmire had made in bringing law and order to their city. They presented him with a gold-topped walking stick and doubled his salary. The next day the El Paso *Lone Star* newspaper reported the shootout under the headline of TWO DEAD IN THREE SECONDS above a photograph of Stoudenmire receiving his award.

'That's a pretty good picture of you there, Dallas,' Doc Cummings complimented the marshal as he sat in his restaurant eating breakfast.

Two Dead in Three Seconds

'Thanks, Doc,' Stoudenmire replied, as he cut into a large slice of ham and dipped it into an egg cooked sunnyside-up. Having chewed it and washed it down with a drink of strong, black coffee, he added with a smirk, 'Seems like we arrived in El Paso just in time to save it from itself.'

Smiling, Doc shared in the joke, but then suddenly became serious.

'Except,' he said, 'not everyone sees it like that.'

'You talking about those Manning brothers?' Stoudenmire remarked.

'Yeah,' Doc agreed.

'Well, I made some enquiries about them. They've been here about a year buying up just about any business that's up for sale.'

'Which makes them think they own the town. And not just the town, I hear. You know the one they call George reckons Belle Starr to be his own?'

'I heard that, too.'

'Well, Belle don't seem to think that and I reckon that's what counts.'

'Sure thing, Dallas. What you gonna do about their saloons and the theatre they own?'

'That's up to them. The council wants them

Two Dead in Three Seconds

closed down but they know they ain't got the power to order it. So they want them tamed.'

'Tamed!' Cummings laughed. 'Tamed! Then they'd better turn the town dry and make it celibate!'

'You're right,' Stoudenmire remarked to his brother-in-law, 'but it's my job now to get over to the Manning brothers the council's point of view.'

'And how you gonna do that?' Cummings asked him. 'And what about Belle's place?'

'She's already got a mind to turn it into a respectable hotel, which is something I aim to help her do. As for the Mannings, well I'll just have to start visiting the Coliseum and the Plaza and making a fuss some.'

'And the Variety Theatre? You really gonna put a stop to those lovely girls on stage flaunting all they got?' Doc asked teasingly.

'No, but maybe I can stop the clientele from roping and dragging them from the stage,' Stoudenmire replied, pouring himself another cup of coffee.

'Why? It ain't nothing but harmless fun.'

'I know that, Doc. But it's what the city council wants and they're paying me handsomely to do it.'

'And what about the Mannings?' Doc asked, his expression suddenly one of earnestness.

'They saw what happened yesterday. It should have been a lesson to them,' Stoudenmire replied.

'And if it ain't?'

'As I said, Doc, I'll just have to start making a fuss.'

Which was exactly what he did. He'd sacked all of Campbell's deputies and appointed a few of his own. He ordered them to start patrolling the streets of the city at night and to arrest anyone caught firing off shots in the saloons. He told them to do the same to anyone caught roping and pulling the girls from the stage in the Variety Theatre. It wasn't long before the Manning brothers were making loud and threatening protests about the matter.

And then one night one of Stoudenmire's deputies was shot at and killed in the Coliseum Saloon. Stoudenmire, who was carousing with Doc Cummings at Belle Starr's hotel, came running. Arriving on the boardwalk outside the saloon, he nearly tripped over the deputy's body, which had simply been removed from the premises and left there. In a rage, he pulled out his gun and stormed through the batwings of the

Two Dead in Three Seconds

saloon and stood just inside firing up into the ceiling. Two of his deputies were with him. As silence fell upon the proceedings, he demanded to know who'd shot his deputy. By now he was well known to like a drink himself and, if challenged, to be fearlessly belligerent. This particular evening, late as it was, he'd had a good skinful.

'I said,' he snarled like a mountain bear with a sore head when no answer came, 'who killed my deputy?'

Tough as most of the men gathered in the saloon were, his rage filled them all with fear. All of them, that was, except George Manning. He stepped forward, drawing on a thin cigar and holding a glass of whiskey.

'Your deputy came in here looking for a fight and got caught in the crossfire of more than he bargained for,' he said to Stoudenmire. 'Ricochets don't pick their targets, they just keep on bouncing around till something soft enough gets in their way and stops them.'

'What, like this?' Stoudenmire replied, pulling his sawn-off belly-gun from his hip pocket, cocking it and pointing it Manning.

'I wouldn't do that if I was you,' a voice from the crowd said.

Stoudenmire looked over to where it had come from and saw Manning's brother Felix pointing a carbine at him.

'Unless you want me to be writing your death certificate,' said another voice, that of Manning's other brother, James, who was a doctor. He was also a hard-drinking fiddle player and was standing now holding his fiddle.

Stoudenmire looked from brother to brother and then back to George Manning.

'This is your saloon, Manning, and it's your responsibility to make sure your customers keep the peace. Now I want the man who fired the shot that killed my deputy to come forward or else I am gonna hold you personally responsible for his death,' he said in uncompromising tones. 'And then I'm gonna close the place down.'

The man who had fired the shot was standing only a few feet away from Stoudenmire. He was the boastful kind and seeing that a stand-off was developing between the big marshal and the Manning brothers reckoned an opportunity to enhance his reputation had just come his way. He also knew that the brothers had talked of giving the marshal what was coming to him and had hoped that he'd be the one hired to do it. Added to this, he'd hired his gun out before to the Manning brothers; he assumed they'd be grateful for its services now. Drunk as he was, his boastful mind made more of his prowess with a gun than was really the case.

'I shot him,' he called out to Stoudenmire, going for his gun at the same time.

Stoudenmire had turned even before anyone else in the room, his deputies included, who were standing with cocked carbines in hand and knew what was going to follow the killer's words. He let the man draw his gun, lightning-fast though his draw was. He even let him raise it and close his finger on the trigger. But then he shot him square between the eyes and, quicker than the time it took the killer to hit the ground, had turned back to face George Manning with his smoking weapon pointing straight at him.

'It was lucky for you, Manning, that he confessed to his crime. Now, any more of my men get hurt here and I will close you down.'

The look on Manning's face gave away nothing of his feelings about the threat Stoudenmire had just made to him, but Stoudenmire knew what he'd be thinking. Just to aggravate the situation a little more, he said to his deputies as he turned to leave the saloon:

'You boys finish things off here while I get back to the Silver Dollar. I got a little lady there who asked me not to be long, and Belle ain't the kind of gal I like to disappoint.'

Everyone in town knew that Stoudenmire had taken Belle Starr from George Manning and nothing he could have said could have humiliated him more in front of his clientele. Though he was unarmed, his brother wasn't. But tough as he was, Felix harboured no illusions about the likes of Stoudenmire, and he was not going to risk pulling a trigger against so formidable a gunman as Dallas had just again proved himself to be. Instead, like his brother George, he became even more determined to get Stoudenmire as soon as ever he could.

FIVE

'Don't you think it's time I sent for Margaret to join me?' Doc Cummings asked Stoudenmire as he ate breakfast the morning after the affair in the Coliseum. Stoudenmire was nursing a hangover.

'You can if you wish, Doc, but I'm not sure I'd advise it yet,' Stoudenmire replied in between taking sips from a cup of black coffee.

'Why's that, Dallas? I think I'm pretty well established here now and could certainly do with the help. I'm getting a little tired of being tied to the place.'

'That's as maybe, but things in this city could go any way, what with the Manning brothers choosing to be at odds with me and the city council. They'd soon get to know she was my sister and I'd hate to think what kinda risk that might put her at,' Stoudenmire replied.

Margaret was his only surviving sister. He'd already lost three to disease and Indians and he wasn't about to take any chances with the one human being in the world he treasured above all.

'You under-estimate that girl, Dallas, I've always told you that. Besides if Belle Starr were to befriend her, as she no doubt would, she'd have nothing to fear from anyone,' Cummings said.

'Well, I'd still like her to stay in San Antonio for a little while longer, while I get things more properly under control.'

Doc Cummings looked at his friend and thought for a while. He'd always been a heavy drinker but since taking on the job of marshal in El Paso and meeting Belle he seemed to be drinking more than ever. He couldn't help but feel that this might have had something to do with his not wanting Margaret coming to El Paso. But, shucks, he couldn't help but think, she was his wife and he wanted her by his side. He was close enough to Stoudenmire to be able to say whatever he thought and he decided to say something now about why he thought he didn't want Margaret to come to El Paso.

Two Dead in Three Seconds

'Doc,' was Stoudenmire's indignant and not a little rattled reply, 'I drink to quench a mighty thirst. That's all. Now, if the good Lord hadn't wanted me to drink so much He wouldn't have given me that mighty thirst. Margaret knows that as well as anyone.'

Doc didn't reply immediately but instead gave his friend a look that asked him who he thought he was kidding. Raising his eyebrows dismissively, Stoudenmire next looked down at his plate and pointedly got on with his breakfast.

'Besides,' he suddenly added, 'I been asked to go help out a community in New Mexico. Seems they got a few heads that need busting over there and no one fit to do it.'

'And what's gonna happen here in El Paso while you're away?' a suddenly concerned Doc asked him.

'That's what I mean,' declared Stoudenmire.

In fact not a lot did happen in El Paso while Stoudenmire was away. He was only gone ten days and what minor outbreaks of trouble there were his deputies were well able to deal with. All but one, that was. It involved Belle Starr and she was able to deal with it herself. Even so, everyone in El Paso knew there'd be hell to pay when

Two Dead in Three Seconds

Stoudenmire got back from New Mexico and found out George Manning had tried to molest the woman Stoudenmire had got used to thinking of as his own. Added to which, Doc Cummings, despite his friend's misgivings, had sent for Margaret and she had wired back to say she was starting out the next day.

Arriving back in El Paso at just after nine in the morning, Stoudenmire's first port of call was the Globe Restaurant. He knew Belle slept usually until after noon and didn't want to spoil her sleep. His surprise was total when, as he walked through the doors of the Globe, he saw Margaret standing by one of the tables.

'Dallas!' she exclaimed on seeing him.

Despite his heavy drinking Stoudenmire always cut a dash and Margaret, despite being his sister, had always been half in love with him.

'Sis!' he replied, at first delighted to see her but then concerned to think she was in town. 'What are you doing in El Paso?'

'Sam sent for me,' Margaret explained, going up to her only surviving relative in the West and kissing him in a sisterly fashion on the cheek. 'A woman's touch has improved things round here, don't you think?' she remarked, looking round

Two Dead in Three Seconds

the restaurant and indicating the starched table-linen and dust-free surfaces of dining-room furniture.

'Well, I suppose they have,' Stoudenmire had to admit, though still feeling and looking a little uneasy. 'Where's Doc?' he asked.

'He's gone somewhere. I'm not quite sure where but he'll be back presently,' Margaret replied. 'Why don't I cook you some breakfast and you can tell me what you were doing over in New Mexico.'

'I am hungry, Margaret,' Stoudenmire admitted, 'but feel I should wash off some of this dust from the trail before I sit down at one of these pretty little tables.'

In reply his sister gave him a knowing smile. She took his hat from him, pulled out a chair from one of the tables and with a nod of the head invited him to sit down.

He was tucking into a plate of ham and eggs when Cummings returned. Stoudenmire, respecting the fact that his friend had a mind of his own, did not berate him for bringing Margaret to the dangerous and uncertain world of El Paso. Nevertheless Cummings felt he had some explaining to do.

Two Dead in Three Seconds

'Things was so quiet after you'd gone, Dallas, and I was so lonely I couldn't help myself,' he said.

'Well, I'm glad to hear the Mannings ain't been no bother,' Stoudenmire remarked, 'exceptin' I always felt their argument was more with me than the city and now that I'm back they'll probably start being an irritant again.'

Cummings hesitated to tell him about the trouble Belle had had with George Manning's making amorous approaches to her in his absence but knew it would be better if he did. If it were left to Belle to tell him he was afraid he might storm out of the Silver Dollar Hotel and into the Coliseum with guns blazing.

'That son of a bitch!' Stoudenmire exclaimed, getting to his feet and kicking the chair he was sitting on out behind him.

'But you don't have to worry,' Doc was quick to point out to him. 'Belle showed him up right and proper in front of the whole city, Dallas, and he hasn't been near her since.'

'I'll kill him!' Stoudenmire exclaimed, striding towards the door of the restaurant.

'Don't,' Margaret begged, getting between him and it. 'You don't need to, Dallas. Doc told you.

Two Dead in Three Seconds

Belle sorted it out for herself. And ain't that Belle? Ain't that just Belle?"

Stoudenmire calmed down and went back to where he'd been sitting. Picking up the chair and throwing it down in front of the table, he sat down on it. No one said anything more and he finished his meal in silence.

His thoughts were still on the matter when later in the day, as dusk was falling, he and Doc were walking north on El Paso Street on the way to his office. On the north-east corner of San Antonio Street was piled a load of bricks in readiness for use in constructing the new State National Bank building. Standing on them holding a double-barrelled shotgun was Bill Johnson, one of George Campbell's former deputy marshals. Once Campbell had gone and Stoudenmire had sacked him, he'd transferred his allegiance to the Manning brothers.

As Stoudenmire and Cummings stepped into the intersection made by El Paso and San Antonio Streets Johnson opened fire. He had never been any good as a deputy marshal, surviving more through inaction than prowess with a gun, and he missed his target. Quick as lightning, both Cummings and Stoudenmire drew their guns and sent Johnson bullet-smacked to his grave. Barely had he hit the ground, when more shots began to ring out. They were coming from the buildings in front and back of them. Cummings ran for cover, squatting down behind the bricks, while Stoudenmire charged headlong towards yellow flashes of light that indicated where the shots were coming from.

One of the men firing those shots was George Manning. Unnerved by the powerful and seemingly indestructible figure of the six foot two, broad-shouldered Stoudenmire coming at him, he decided to make a run for it. He came out of his dark corner with guns blazing. Stoudenmire would still have remained unscathed had not a ricocheting bullet smashed into his left heel, sending him stumbling to the ground. Seeing his chance, Manning levelled his gun to plug him full of hot lead. Seeing this, Doc Cummings broke cover and standing taller than his five-foot-eight frame should have allowed, riddled Manning's chest and belly with .45s from his ivory-handled, engraved Colt Peacemakers. By now the remainder of Manning's accomplices had fled the scene.

'You all right?' he asked of Stoudenmire, rushing up to him but taking the precaution of scan-

Two Dead in Three Seconds

ning the shadowy doors and alleyways all around.

'Yes, I am,' replied an uncowed if hurting Stoudenmire. 'Thanks to you, Doc.'

'Think nothing of it, partner,' Cummings replied. It was clear to him there was no one left hiding in the shadows and that the fight was over. For the moment, anyway. 'Reckon we'd better get you to a doctor,' he advised his friend, helping him up.

'Well, he won't be bothering Belle no more,' Stoudenmire remarked, catching sight of Manning's body as it lay in a vast pool of blood that drained quickly into the dirt of the street.

'Marshal!' the voice of one of Stoudenmire's deputies exclaimed as he suddenly appeared on the scene, preventing Cummings from answering. 'You hurt bad?'

'Just a bullet in the heel,' Stoudenmire replied, feeling his boot getting sticky with blood. 'Help Doc here get me to the Silver Dollar and then you can go get me a doctor.'

Another deputy who'd come running was instructed to go on to the Coliseum and tell whichever of Manning's brothers was there to fetch an undertaker to collect his body. As all this was going on, Cummings could not help but reflect on what a narrow escape he and Stoudenmire had had. Then his thoughts turned to the fact that it had been him who had killed George Manning. The brothers would now be gunning for him, too. He couldn't help but wish he had taken his best friend's advice and left Margaret where she was, far away and out of harm's reach in San Antonio.

SIX

For their own good Felix and James Manning had to be seen to distance themselves from their dead brother's attempt on the life of the city marshal. Had they not done so, the city council would have had their places shut down and they'd have been run out of town. But secretly they planned their revenge. While they did so a problem that had not gone away suddenly came to a head all over again. The Mexican *vaqueros* appeared in town claiming that hundreds of their cattle were still being rustled and demanding satisfaction.

'We know who is taking our cattle and we want something done about it,' their leader warned Stoudenmire on the steps of the boardwalk that led to his office.

There were maybe fifty or more *vaqueros* looking mean and hungry for a fight. Stoudenmire's heel wound had barely healed itself and he wasn't as nimble on his feet as he liked himself to be.

'Look,' he said to the leader, whose name was Francisco Fernandez, 'why don't you come inside and tell me what you know and then we can try and get to the bottom of it.'

Fernandez, who had not forgotten the way Stoudenmire had shot down John Hale some months before, trusted him and agreed to what was suggested.

'Tell your men to go back to Mexico and wait for you. It'll be safer that way.'

The Mexican looked at Stoudenmire, uncertain that he should take the risk of leaving himself so exposed in the gringos part of town. He knew that there were those in El Paso who would dearly love to see Stoudenmire dead and he didn't want anyone like the son of John Hale, the person he considered to be behind the rustling of Mexican cattle and a known friend of the Mannings, to use a fight with the marshal as cover to gun him down.

'Pedro, Juan, Carlos, you stay. The rest of you go wait for me at Rosa's Cantina,' he ordered his men.

Two Dead in Three Seconds

Stoudenmire caught the eye of Fernandez and nodded his acceptance of the Mexican's action. Standing back he gestured to him to go before him into his office. As Fernandez accepted his offer the three *vaqueros* he had told to stay behind took up defensive positions on the boardwalk outside the marshal's office.

'Coffee?' Stoudenmire asked Fernandez, lifting a pot from a stove in a corner of his office.

'*Gracias*,' Fernandez replied.

Taking his own tin mug, Stoudenmire threw the dregs of his last mug of coffee on to the floor. Then he got a clean mug for Fernandez and filled them both with fresh coffee.

'Reckon you might like a drop of this?' Stoudenmire remarked, opening a drawer and taking out a bottle of good rye whiskey.

Smiling, Fernandez pushed his mug towards the marshal. He liked Stoudenmire, as did all Mexicans in and around El Paso. They thought him fair and, of course, over-blessed with *machismo*, the only thing in the eyes of all Latinos that made a man what he was.

Both men drank from their mugs of heavily whiskey-laced coffee, eyeing one another in businesslike fashion. Then Fernandez spoke.

'Marshal, you did a good job in ridding this town of Campbell, Hale and then George Manning. All decent people thank you for it, Mexican and gringo alike. But unless you stop our cattle being stolen you are going to have trouble of a different kind on your hands. I cannot hold my people back any longer. Josh Hale has taken up where his father left off. You know that and now you must do something about it.'

'I am the city marshal, Fernandez, not the US marshal,' Stoudenmire attempted to explain to the leader of the *vaqueros*. 'The job you are asking me to do is the responsibility of Texas Rangers, not me.'

'Texas Rangers!' Fernandez spat contemptuously. 'Texas Rangers! What help they ever give my people, eh? None.'

Stoudenmire could not help but agree with what the Mexican was saying. Far from helping to bring law and order to El Paso, the Texas Rangers had criticized him for gunning down George Campbell.

'Well,' he smirked, 'I don't have much use for those thirty-dollars-a-month sons of bitches myself. But that doesn't alter the fact that outside the city limits they're the law.'

Two Dead in Three Seconds

Stoudenmire could see that he was disappointing the leader of the *vaqueros*, who he knew might go on to take the law into his own hands and start a border war.

'I'll tell you what I'll do,' he said to him. 'I'll send a telegram to the commander of the Texas Rangers in Austin and tell him what's going on down here. But I promise you if he don't send someone to put paid to Josh Hale and his accomplices then I *will* do it myself. I guarantee you that.'

Fernandez, who, though he had no faith in the Texas Rangers, did respect Stoudenmire's word, decided to let him give it a try.

'How long this gonna take?' he asked him.

'Two days, three at the most,' was Stoudenmire's reply.

'OK,' Fernandez agreed. 'But no longer, Marshal. No longer,' he repeated, looking grave and every inch the leader of his people.

Stoudenmire saw Fernandez out of his office and watched him and his men ride down El Paso Street to cross the line into Mexico. Then he turned back into his office, sat down at his desk and reached for pen and paper. Addressing himself to General W.H. King, Austin commander of the Texas Rangers, he began to write . . .

. . . a lot of rangers stationed in this portion of the state have run most ingloriously when called to the scratch. I have found them untrustworthy and unreliable . . . more ready to aggravate than to preserve the public peace. They take sides with the lawless rather than the law-abiding section of this town . . .

Continuing, he spelt out the precise problem relating to the Mexicans and warned of dire consequences if something was not done right away. Then he took the letter to the telegraph office and asked the clerk to send it.

It was forty-eight hours before a reply was received from Austin. When it did arrive it was not the reply Stoudenmire had hoped for but was more or less what he'd expected. The General said he had every faith in the Rangers already deployed in the area. However, he added, he would inform the officer in charge of Stoudenmire's concerns. This told Stoudenmire what he had to do next. And if General W.H. King and his Texas Rangers didn't like it, they could kiss his ass.

'Fernandez,' he informed the leader of the

Two Dead in Three Seconds

vaqueros less than an hour after the telegraph boy had delivered the reply from Austin. 'I am going to make you and your men deputy marshals and then we're gonna go and get your cattle back.'

Fernandez gave him a look of incredulity.

'You got a reply to your telegram to the commander of the Rangers?' he said.

'Yes,' replied Stoudenmire.

'And you no like?'

'No,' answered Stoudenmire.

'I thought so,' remarked the leader of the *vaqueros*. 'But Marshal, Mexicans from across the border, deputies? Is that legal?'

'You let me worry about that.'

Fernandez looked uncertain.

'Look, Fernandez,' Stoudenmire said to him, leaning forward on his desk. 'Do you want your cattle back or not?'

Fernandez looked at him for a moment and then thought: if this was how a Yankee lawman wanted to deal with the matter, then OK, he'd go along with it. Added to which, he knew his men would get the kick of their lives out of wearing gringo deputy marshal's badges.

Stoudenmire in fact had a job producing fifty

badges, but the city's blacksmith was more than obliging. Riding off to the Hale ranch he and his deputies in their sombreros and silver-decorated saddles and stirrups cut a fine if somewhat unlikely posse of men.

'What do you think he is up to?' James Manning asked, as he watched Stoudenmire and the Mexicans ride out of El Paso.

'Seems obvious to me,' his brother Felix replied. 'It's gotta be cattle. Someone ought to ride out and warn Josh.'

'Can't be legal, though, Mexicans being sworn in as deputies. Texas Rangers won't like it, of that you can be sure,' James Manning remarked.

'Well, best we inform them, then. I'll get Scoot to ride out and warn Josh. You make sure the Rangers find out.'

'Sure thing,' replied James. 'And, brother,' he added, 'while Stoudenmire's out of the way maybe we oughtta pay that friend of his a visit.'

A wicked smile spread across Felix's face.

'Yeah,' he replied. 'It's time that son of a bitch paid the price for killing George.'

*

Two Dead in Three Seconds

Later that day when the two brothers called in at the Globe Restaurant looking for Cummings he was not in. Margaret was though. Without any fear she walked straight up to them and asked what they wanted, adding, 'I don't suppose you dropped in to sample my cooking.'

'Business with your husband, ma'am,' James had replied, as he and his brother put on a show of politely doffing their hats.

'Well, as you can see, he's not here,' she informed them, her voice full of contempt.

It was an unwritten rule in the West that you didn't take out a man's wrongdoing on his woman and so the brothers left. Cummings, when he returned, became incensed to think they'd had the nerve to come looking for him in the place that doubled as his home. Added to this, he had not been taken in by the Mannings' stance that they'd had nothing to do with their brother's attempt on his and Stoudenmire's lives. For some time he had wanted to tell them so. He decided now was the time. Margaret begged him to wait until Stoudenmire returned.

'Dallas's hands are tied by the wishes of the city council but mine ain't. And besides, I ain't having them thinking they can walk into here whenever they like and get away with it,' he remonstrated with her, strapping on his six-guns and making sure they were fully loaded.

'Samuel, don't,' Margaret pleaded with him one more time. 'Please wait until Dallas gets back in town.'

'Honey,' he replied, 'they only came here because he was out of town. I gotta show them I can protect myself, otherwise who knows what they'll try next.'

Margaret was not convinced but knew she couldn't stop him doing what he felt he had to do. But his goodbye kiss filled her with a dark foreboding and when he'd gone she locked the door on the restaurant and hurried over to Belle Starr.

Doc was going to the Coliseum. It was dusk. He found James Manning sitting in a high chair at the bar leaning back and smoking a cigar.

'Manning,' he snarled at him, 'I've come to tell you to stay away from my restaurant.'

Manning didn't flinch a muscle. Instead he took the cigar from his mouth and looking at it said, 'Oh yeah?'

'And what's more,' Cummings added, 'you ain't fooled me one bit. I know you had a hand in your brother trying to kill me and Stoudenmire.'

Two Dead in Three Seconds

'Is that so?' Manning replied, getting down from his chair. 'Well, why don't you just step outside and say it?'

He was armed with a Remington .44.

'Suits me,' was all Cummings said in reply. He knew he was quick on the draw and James Manning had no reputation for being so.

Outside they both walked to the centre of El Paso Street and took up their positions.

'Now, what'd you say back there?' Manning asked. As he stood with his legs apart and his right hand hovering over his gun, he suddenly began to wonder if he'd done a wise thing asking Cummings out to draw.

'I said,' replied Cummings, 'I know you had a hand in your brother trying to kill me and Stoudenmire.'

'Your brother-in-law, the marshal of this fair city,' Manning retorted, 'stole his gal. I'd say George had a right to try and take her back. But it was his fight. Why would I want to get involved?'

Men who'd been drinking in the Coliseum had begun to congregate on the boardwalk outside, hoping to see some action. It made both Cummings and Manning feel uneasy, not least because it shut out what little light there was and now they could barely see more than the outline of one another.

' 'Cause you liked to think you ruled this town before Stoudenmire came along and now you know you don't.'

'Well, if that's all it is,' said Manning, 'why don't we save this until the marshal gets back? After all, he's the lawman around here, I thought, not you. I mean you ain't been sworn in as one of his deputies, have you, like half of Mexico?'

Cummings peered through the dark at Manning, uncertain of what he was playing at.

'You calling this off, then, Manning?' he asked.

'Sure am,' Manning replied. 'I mean, we ain't got anything to fight about. I'm a doctor and you're a rest'raunter. Ain't that about it?'

Cummings wasn't convinced but he felt he knew better than to draw on a man he could hardly see. He also began to wonder where the other brother, Felix, might be.

'OK,' he replied. 'But I want a drink and I want it on the house.'

'Fine by me,' Manning replied, indicating with his left hand that Cummings should be his guest and precede him back into the Coliseum.

Two Dead in Three Seconds

Sam Cummings was considering taking up Manning's offer when someone suddenly pushed their way through the crowd gathered on the boardwalk. It was Belle Starr and she was carrying a carbine. Margaret was behind her.

'Why,' exclaimed James Manning, 'if it ain't the whore of El Paso herself! You taken up arms again, Belle? Don't you find them petticoat weeds of yours a hindrance when it comes to doing a man's work?'

'Drop your gun, James,' Belle snarled at Manning, 'or else.'

'Or else what?' Manning sneered at her, turning away as if to seek a laugh from the men gathered on the boardwalk.

Belle was about to show him what when he suddenly drew his gun and rolling on the ground fired at Cummings. Once and then a second time. As he did so Belle fired at him but he rolled across the street into the dark and her shots missed. She was stopped from taking any further action by Margaret's pushing past her and running to her husband.

'Samuel, Samuel,' Margaret moaned, throwing herself down beside him. He was lying spread-eagled in the dirt, two slugs in his chest. She

Two Dead in Three Seconds

began to take him in her arms, but as she did so he let out a bloodcurdling groan and breathed his last.

Belle ran down the steps of the boardwalk to where Cummings lay.

'Son of a gun,' she growled, peering into the dark, followed by, 'James Manning, wherever you are, you're dead meat.' Then she turned on the crowd and barked at them an order to disappear. Frightened by her fury and the reputation that had preceded her move to El Paso, they all turned and began to file back into the saloon.

'I'm sorry, Margaret, I'm really very sorry,' she said tenderly, turning to the woman she already thought of as her sister-in-law, though not being so careless as to take her eyes from the dark that hid the far side of the street.

SEVEN

Stoudenmire led the Mexican *vaqueros* straight to the herd of cattle grazing the Hale ranch. He had no intention of confronting the deceased John Hale's son Josh. Instead he had decided he was simply going to let the *vaqueros* cut from the herd as many cattle as they reckoned had been stolen from them, which was some three hundred steers. There were only a handful of cowboys watching the herd and they could not believe their eyes when they saw Stoudenmire and his deputies ride up and in a very businesslike fashion start helping themselves to a large section of the herd. There was no foreman amongst them but the cowboy who was nominally in charge rode up to Stoudenmire and asked him what he thought he was doing.

'I'm allowing these men to take back what's theirs,' Stoudenmire replied sternly. He'd brought his mount to a halt and was sitting astride it holding a Winchester butt-end menacingly against a thigh and pointing skywards.

'But you can't do that,' the cowboy replied. 'These are Hale's cattle. They've got his brand on them.'

'We're doing it, son,' Stoudenmire said. 'And I wouldn't try stopping us, if I were you, unless you want more trouble than you can handle.'

Stoudenmire was not unknown to the cowboy and he knew that he was capable of killing them all if he took a mind to. Without saying another word he reined his mount around and rode back to talk to the other cowboys, who were by now gathered in a cluster questioning one another as to what was going on.

'That's Stoudenmire, ain't it?' one of the men said to the cowboy in charge as he drew up beside them.

'Sure is,' the cowboy replied.

'What we gonna do about it?'

'Nothing,' the cowboy in charge replied. 'He ain't the kind of man you mess with. I'm gonna ride back to the homeplace and tell Josh what's going on down here. You all just stay here and watch. Don't try nothing until I get back with Josh and the rest of the boys. Then we'll see what's what.'

'He's what?' Josh Hale asked incredulously when informed by the cowboy of what was happening. 'He's stealing my cattle? Stoudenmire and a bunch of Mexicans?'

'He says they're taking back what's rightfully theirs,' the cowboy reiterated.

'He does, does he? Right, Dick,' Hale declared, dropping what he was doing. 'Tell the men to get ready to ride. We got us some cattle thieves to sort out.'

'There was a lot of them, Josh,' Dick warned him. 'Maybe fifty or more.'

'There's a lot of us. Go round 'em up. And tell Jim to issue them with plenty of ammo.'

Jim, Jim Ford, was Hale's foreman. He'd been his father's foreman and had always played a big part in the rustling of Mexican cattle. He'd never hesitated to kill any *vaquero* who got in his way and Josh knew he wouldn't now. Added to which he hated Stoudenmire for killing John Hale.

It only took minutes for the Hale ranch hands to get mounted and ready to ride. Josh Hale and

Two Dead in Three Seconds

Jim Ford were at their head as they galloped full pelt for the herd. They came in on the Mexicans, letting rip a storm of lead. But the Mexicans were ready for them. As the remainder of the herd scattered, the Mexicans stampeded those they'd cut out, while firing over their shoulders at the pursuing cowboys.

'Spread out, men,' Jim Ford called out, as some of his men began to fall.

Stoudenmire had not joined in with the herding of the cattle and was watching from a safe distance. It gave him the greatest of pleasure to see the cowboys falling. They'd all been involved in the rustling of Mexican beeves and now they were paying the price.

Josh Hale and Jim Ford looked around but could see no sign of the marshal.

'They're getting away,' Ford called out to Hale, pulling up close beside him.

'Let 'em,' Hale called back, as their horses kept up a gallop. 'We're losing too many men, anyway. Don't see any sign of Stoudenmire, do you?'

As he finished asking the question a bullet zinged between them. Both men turned to find out exactly where the marshal was. He was a few hundred yards behind, firing at them with his

Two Dead in Three Seconds

Winchester. Hale pulled a gun and started firing back.

'You keep him occupied,' Ford called out, 'while I call back the men.'

Half the Hale ranch cowboys had been brought down by now and the others were glad to be called off. Seeing what was happening, Fernandez called some of his men to follow him and they gave chase, leaving the rest to carry on driving the herd to Mexico. When he caught sight of Stoudenmire riding and firing at the cowboys, while appearing to be immune to their return fire, he could barely believe his eyes.

Seeing the Mexicans coming, Ford and Hale soon realized their situation was hopeless. Hale was still young and his first thought was to run and save his skin. But Jim Ford, who'd lived a long and full life, which, thanks to Stoudenmire, he now felt had run its course, was determined to make the man pay.

'Take the others and make a run for it,' he ordered his old boss's only son, 'while I create a diversion.'

'I ain't going anywhere without you,' Hale called back over the din of the gunfire bursting all around them.

Two Dead in Three Seconds

'Don't be stupid, Josh. There's too many of them. Just go and leave me to get Stoudenmire.'

As the Mexicans drew closer and the air thickened with the whistling of bullets, Hale decided Ford was right and, pulling his horse around to ride off west, he dug in his spurs and slackened the reins of his mount. His men soon followed, firing at the Mexicans as they went.

'Yah!' yelled Ford and charged his horse headlong at Stoudenmire, who brought his own mount to a halt.

Ford was firing as he came, his range getting surer, but still no bullets hit Stoudenmire. Then his cylinder was empty. As he threw the gun aside in disgust, he saw Stoudenmire lift his Winchester to his right shoulder and begin to take aim.

'Yah, yah!' he yelled at his horse, riding now in a blind rage straight for Stoudenmire, intending to drag him from his saddle. He was only a few feet away from him, certain, as he reckoned it, to achieve his objective, when the marshal pulled the trigger and hit him straight between the eyes. The impact of the bullet sent him flying from his horse, which, free now to follow its instincts, was able to wheel right at the last

Two Dead in Three Seconds

moment and avoid Stoudenmire.

Fernandez and his *vaqueros* saw what had happened and their admiration for this gringo braveheart knew no bounds.

'This is a great thing you have done for us,' Fernandez said to him later, 'and we Mexicans will never forget you for it.'

Before Stoudenmire could reply he and the Mexicans suddenly became aware of a group of men riding hell for leather towards them. It soon became apparent who they were.

'This spells trouble,' Fernandez remarked.

'Leave it to me,' the marshal replied.

'What in God's name has been going on here?' the leader of what was a company of Texas Rangers snarled at Stoudenmire as he and his men pulled up in front of him.

The marshal immediately sensed the man's antagonism towards him and guessed he'd received word from General King in Austin.

'There were stolen Mexican cattle on the Hale ranch and me and my deputies here came to get 'em,' he informed him.

'Your deputies? the leader of the Texas Rangers asked.

'Yeah.'

Two Dead in Three Seconds

'But they're all Mexicans and only US citizens are eligible to be US deputy marshals.'

'El Paso Mexicans,' Stoudenmire replied.

'Who says?'

'I do, and the city council.'

The leader of the Rangers knew exactly who Stoudenmire was and he knew he had to tread carefully. But he hated Mexicans and had hoped that here was an opportunity to hang a few.

'Well,' he declared. 'I'm gonna have to take these Mexicans in until I have investigated things further.'

His words made Fernandez and his men immediately raise their weapons. In response the Texas Rangers did the same. Neither side fired a shot but easily would if provoked further.

'You can try to, if you like,' Stoudenmire replied. 'But, as you can see, they may not be too co-operative about it.'

The leader of the Texas Rangers looked from Stoudenmire to the Mexicans and back again. His men followed suit. The air was thick with tension, with each side fearful the other might start something that, at such close range, could only mean certain death for most of them. Stoudenmire felt he knew the calibre of Texas

Two Dead in Three Seconds

Ranger that policed this part of Texas and he didn't rate them highly.

'Right,' said the leader, after what seemed like an age of deliberation, 'you seem to have the matter in hand, Stoudenmire. We'll leave you to deal with it.'

'That's probably the best idea,' Stoudenmire replied.

'Wouldn't waste too much time on it, though,' the Texas Ranger said matter-of-factly, as he turned his horse to ride away, 'your brother-in-law was killed yesterday. Better get back to El Paso before the killer gets clean away.'

'What d'you say?' a stunned Stoudenmire asked him.

The Texas Ranger was already leading his men away and didn't stop to repeat what he'd said. In fact Stoudenmire didn't need him to. He'd heard. The Texas Rangers could go. They'd be of no use to him here, in El Paso, or anywhere. He could forget them. He looked at Fernandez.

'I gotta get back to El Paso. You'd better ride with me and cross the border there,' he said.

'Sure thing, Marshal,' Fernandez replied. 'But if there's trouble in the city we stay and help you,' he added in comradely tones.

Two Dead in Three Seconds

'Yeah, thanks,' was all Stoudenmire said in reply, as he turned his horse and began to ride in the direction of El Paso, his mind already struggling with the fact that what the Texas Ranger had told him was probably true. His thoughts were then for Margaret. Becoming fearful for her safety, he spurred his horse into a trot and then a gallop. He gave it no rest until they reached El Paso a few hours later.

EIGHT

'He ain't been seen anywhere since,' Belle told Stoudenmire.

He'd gone straight to the Globe Restaurant and not finding his sister there had gone to the Silver Dollar Hotel.

'He killed him in cold blood,' Margaret sobbed into her brother's chest.

'He's maintaining it was a fair shoot-out and so are all his customers,' remarked Belle, 'and the city councillors seem to want to believe him.'

'I thought you said he ain't been seen.'

'He ain't, Dallas, but that's the word that's come back. He won't show his face until he knows the matter's settled one way or another with you. That he knows can only be done through the city council.'

Two Dead in Three Seconds

'Best I go see them, then.'

'Dallas, can't we just pack up and go back to San Antonio?' Margaret asked.

'This is my town and I ain't being driven out of it by no one,' her brother replied. 'What about Felix Manning? What's he had to say for himself?'

'He's been shooting his mouth off everywhere, saying Doc got what he deserved for killing George. I tell you, Dallas, there ain't gonna be any peace in this town until those Manning brothers are either run out or killed,' Belle argued.

'You're right, Belle. They've been trouble ever since I put on the badge,' Stoudenmire replied.

'I told him to wait until you got back,' Margaret sobbed.

'The council's made it illegal to carry a gun, fight, drink, gamble, swear or disturb the peace in any way within the city limits,' Belle informed him.

'Ha!' laughed Stoudenmire. 'As if making laws made cities fine places to live in!'

He suddenly looked black as thunder. His best friend was dead and his sister was dressed in widow's weeds. He remembered that he'd warned Doc not to send for Margaret and now this had

Two Dead in Three Seconds

happened. She'd seen him gunned down.

'Right,' he suddenly declared, 'I'm gonna turn this town upside down until I find James Manning. And when I do find him he's gonna pay.'

He'd grabbed a bottle of whiskey when he'd stepped into the Silver Dollar Hotel and he'd already drunk half of it. As he spoke he took a slug and consumed nearly half of what was left. He'd be coming tanked up and full of a whiskey-drinker's rage; the low life of El Paso would know it had better run for cover. His first call, though, was going to be on the mayor.

'Don't you think it's time you and the Mannings got together to settle your differences?' Mayor Solomon Schultz said.

Stoudenmire had arrived in his office having walked down El Paso Street waving his guns and calling James Manning to come out and face him like a man. It had distressed the good citizens of El Paso and they had hurried to get out of his way.

'What?' the marshal roared. 'I thought I was appointed to clean up this town.'

'You were,' the mayor agreed, 'and we are grateful to you for all that you've done to achieve that end, but this feud between you and the Manning brothers is making citizens of this city feel very frightened. It's become personal and we have just witnessed that it can explode into gunfire at any moment.'

'And that wasn't happening before I came along?'

'I ain't telling you how to do you job, Marshal, I'm just saying you and the Mannings have got to settle your differences. Samuel Cummings went to the Coliseum looking for trouble. The Mannings and everyone else who was there and saw it are saying that James Manning drew in self-defence—'

'That's not what Miss Starr and his wife are saying,' interrupted Stoudenmire.

'Yeah, well, Miss Starr didn't exactly help matters any, according to witnesses.'

The mayor might have had more to say about Belle Starr, whose own reputation as companion to thieves and killers was already legendary in the West, even if it was something which, in coming to El Paso, she had been trying to play down. But he knew that she and Stoudenmire had struck up a romantic association together and he knew it would not be tactful.

Two Dead in Three Seconds

'Seems to me,' replied Stoudenmire, 'things might have been a darn sight worse if she had not been there.'

'Well, either way, things have gotta alter now, Marshal. Settlers are being put off coming to El Paso and business is suffering as a result. I suggest you and the Mannings get together in my chambers and we'll try and sort things out.'

Stoudenmire was incredulous at what he was hearing but realized that if he wanted to keep his job he had to go along with it.

'OK, mayor,' he agreed. 'I'll meet with those sons of bitches but I ain't gonna forget one of them killed Doc and that my sister has lost her husband. If you can persuade me to shake hands with the man that did that, there'll be peace. But if you can't, I won't answer for what the outcome of any meeting between me and the Mannings might be. In the meantime I still gotta job to do and if James Manning or his brother get in my way they'll pay the price.'

Stoudenmire's words did not fill the mayor with much hope that things could be sorted out at a meeting of the two parties but he nevertheless felt they could not be left to go on as they were.

'I hear you passed a new law banning people

from doing just about anything,' Stoudenmire remarked.

'Only what can lead to trouble,' the mayor replied, adding pointedly, 'a little sobriety would not go amiss in this city.'

The point the mayor was obviously trying to make was not lost on Stoudenmire but he made no reply. He decided his meeting with the mayor was over and made to leave. The city council could employ him or not, he didn't really care. The look he gave the mayor in saying goodbye made this clear. Pulling the door of the mayor's office shut behind him, Stoudenmire reminded himself just how dependent on men like him the peace of the West was.

As the mayor watched him from his office window take strong, bold strides down the boardwalk, he knew the city should be grateful to Stoudenmire but at the same time he feared the consequences of his methods.

'Give me another bottle of whiskey,' was how Belle was greeted by Stoudenmire, as he stepped back into the Silver Dollar Hotel.

'Sure thing, honey,' she replied, thinking it was just as well Margaret was not there. 'How'd things go with the mayor?' she asked, though from the look of him she could tell. His reply was not what she expected.

'Belle, you and I have gotta get married.'

Belle looked at him and thought for a moment. She knew how deeply unhappy he was over Doc's death but it seemed to her his reaction properly ought to be to seek revenge, not to settle down. What indeed had passed between him and the mayor?

'Dallas?' she asked. 'Did I hear you right? Married?'

'Yeah,' he replied, filling a shot-glass for a second time and knocking it back.

'And what about the Mannings?' she asked.

'What about the Mannings?' Stoudenmire roared.

'I see,' replied Belle, who could guess now what had gone down in the mayor's office. 'OK,' she said. 'Dallas Stoudenmire, I will marry you, though I ain't changing my profession any more than I imagine you're gonna change yours.'

'Right,' agreed Stoudenmire, taking the whiskey-bottle in hand. 'It's agreed then.'

He walked up to Belle and stood before her. Looking into his eyes, Belle could see all the hurt that was eating him up inside over the death of Doc. She wondered for how long he'd be able to keep it bottled up. She guessed the mayor had told him the verdict was that James Manning had shot in self-defence. The editorials in the El Paso *Lone Star* had been calling for the city to either sack Stoudenmire or back him and let him get on with cleaning up the city. *Now, it had said, is not the time to discuss the right or wrong of past issues. Tale bearers and agitators must be made to understand that their services are not wanted and their interference in the running of this city will not be permitted.* Fine words, but she knew how many of the senior citizens of El Paso the Mannings had in their pockets. This fact alone dictated what constraints the city council would try to put on Stoudenmire, never mind what the good citizens demanded. Marriage to her, she realized, was his answer to that.

She continued looking into his eyes and he into hers. He had consumed a lot of alcohol but he was not drunk. She knew this. He'd shoot up the town some on his way back to his office. And he'd holler and curse the Manning brothers. But in the morning he'd be sober and then he'd get on with the real task of his job as marshal and sooner or

Two Dead in Three Seconds

later someone would pay for the death of his best friend and brother-in-law.

NINE

'He's gotta be stopped, Felix. Jim's dead, them Mexicans took half the herd and the rest has been scattered. He's gotta be stopped.'

It was Josh Hale; he and Felix Manning were in one of the back rooms of the Coliseum.

'Have you been to see the Rangers?' Felix asked. He was standing with his back to Hale, looking out of a grimy widow into a grubby alley.

'I came across 'em out in the scrub. They said they ought to arrest me for rustling Mexican cattle.'

'What d'you say to that?'

'I asked them if they was serious and when they said no I rode off and came straight here. Where's James?'

'Hiding out some place but he'll be back tomorrow. They want us to meet with Stoudenmire to try and settle our differences.'

'You going to?' asked an incredulous Josh Hale. He was still only a kid, barely old enough to be playing a man's game. He was fine rustling Mexican cattle at night and firing off a gun into the dark, while the older cowboys did the real fighting and killing of Mexicans. But a real fight in broad daylight with men all around him being killed had unnerved him and he didn't know where to run.

'Reckon we ain't got much choice, if we're gonna carry on doing business in El Paso,' replied Felix, who had turned away from the window and was now facing Hale.

'But what about George? Stoudenmire killed him.'

'Yeah, and James killed Cummings. Guess that kinda squares things up some.'

Josh Hale looked confused.

'I lost my daddy and now Jim's dead. What am I supposed to do?' he asked Felix, needing reassurance from someone he could look up to. The Manning brothers were years older than him and they'd made a success of things in El Paso. Or at least they had until Stoudenmire pinned on the marshal's badge. They'd been friends with his

Two Dead in Three Seconds

father and they'd all made money, and fast. He looked up to them and expected them to help him now.

Felix thought for a moment and then replied:

'Go back to the ranch, son. Round up the cattle and then wait. Stoudenmire ain't interested in you. The Mexicans were threatening to make trouble in town, so he helped them get back their rustled cattle. But there's plenty more where they came from. We can replace them. Just sit tight for a while, until things quieten down a bit. When we've had our meeting with Stoudenmire we'll ride out and let you know how things stand. In the meantime we'll find you another foreman.'

Josh Hale looked relieved to think he wasn't after all on his own; that his father's friends were there to look out for him.

'OK,' he said managing a smile, if a short-lived one. The absence of one on Felix Manning's face reminded him that there still wasn't in reality anything to smile about. And if he could have read his mind, he'd have realized he was being fooled. Manning's only concern was the ranch and the herd, in which he and his brother had a big enough stake to want to make sure a setback did not turn into a disaster.

'Go now,' he said to the boy in suitably avuncular tones, 'before our friend the marshal gets wind of the fact you're here.'

The boy did as he was told, opening a back door and looking carefully up and down the alley to make sure he wasn't going to be seen before hurrying off to where he'd left his horse. His departure left Manning deep in thought. Mainly about the big bribe they'd paid to the Texas Rangers to turn a blind eye to their cross-border activities. He'd better inform them, he thought, that the young Hale was now a liability to their whole operation and that he should be dealt with accordingly.

'God damn it, Sol,' James Manning remonstrated with Mayor Schultz at the meeting arranged between him and his brother and Stoudenmire, 'he took a bunch of Mexicans out to the Hale ranch and stood and watched them steal their cattle. And when Jim Ford tried to stop them he shot him dead.'

Stoudenmire had already had his say about the cattle being rustled from south of the border. He despised the Manning brothers, and James Manning in particular for the killing of Doc, and hearing them now tell more of their damn lies and untruths he didn't know why he didn't just simply pull a gun and kill them where they sat. Didn't he owe Doc at least that?

'Gentlemen,' Mayor Schultz, exasperated by the entrenched attitudes of the two parties, suddenly declared, 'we are not getting anywhere arguing to and fro like this. And I gotta tell all of you that unless you can resolve your grievances here today, the city council is going to have to take matters into its own hands to ensure that your quarrel does not again endanger the peace of this city.'

Knowing whatever peace they made wouldn't be worth a light, the Mannings and Stoudenmire decided they might just as well say and do whatever the mayor asked them to, if only to escape from one another's loathsome presence. The silence that fell upon both parties deluded the mayor into believing they were prepared to see reason at last.

'Good,' he said. 'Now I have here a treaty the city council has drawn up for you both to sign and anyone that breaks it will be fined heavily or else drummed out of town. Read it, gentlemen, and be sure it's understood before you sign it. There can be no going back once you have.'

Stoudenmire read it first and then handed it to James Manning. It read:

We, the undersigned parties, having this day settled all our differences and unfriendly feelings existing between us, hereby agree that we will hereafter meet and pass each other on friendly terms, and that bygones shall be bygones, and that we shall never allude in the future to any past animosities between us.

'You have both lost a brother, gentlemen,' Mayor Shultz reminded them, taking a pen and dipping it into an inkwell, 'let us hope this will bring an end to it.'

Holding the pen out in front of him, he hoped one of them would take it. Both parties thought the document naïve in the extreme and saw no harm in signing it. Despite his ambitions as revealed to Belle Starr, Stoudenmire was not in fact in any way a political animal and would not have lowered himself to be the first to reach for the mayor's pen. James Manning was different. He hoped one day to stand for office and thought the right kind of gesture now would pay dividends in the future. Taking the proffered pen from the mayor's hand, his was the first signature to appear on the peace treaty. The mayor would have liked a photograph for the paper and indeed a reporter from the El Paso *Lone Star* was on hand but Stoudenmire could not be persuaded to shake the hand of the man responsible for the cold-blooded killing of his friend and brother-in-law, Doc Cummings. James Manning had offered his right hand but the marshal had simply glared at him. So emphatic was the rebuff that the idea was quickly dropped.

Well, if there's nothing more, Mayor,' Stoudenmire declared, 'I have a city to police. Good day!'

As he turned to leave the mayor's office, he suddenly stopped. 'By the way,' he said, 'I thought you might like to know there's gonna be a wedding. Mine and Belle's. Francisco Fernandez has agreed to be my best man. Now ain't that something?'

Without waiting for a reaction he turned and left. The Mannings and Mayor Schultz were speechless as they watched him go. 'Son of a gun' were the only words that were uttered. They

Two Dead in Three Seconds

issued from the lips of James Manning but they echoed the thoughts of all three men. Stoudenmire's words were having the desired effect, just as he knew they would.

TEN

'We lost fifty head of cattle last night.'

It was Fernandez's right-hand man, Jose.

'And men?' Fernandez asked.

'Two dead and six wounded.'

'And theirs?'

'More. We killed the wounded they left behind.'

Fernandez thought for a moment. He knew who was stealing their cattle and he knew that the Texas Rangers were doing nothing about it. He could cross the border and steal back his cattle as before but his scouts told him the Hale ranch was now so heavily guarded they'd find it much harder than they had the first time, when the element of surprise was on their side. He decided he'd have to go and see his friend Marshal Dallas Stoudenmire and hear what he suggested. He was proud to think the marshal had asked him to be his best man but he knew the risks it involved for both of them. There were many people now, and not just the Manning brothers, who would gladly put a bullet in their backs.

'Jose, get the men ready to ride. We'll go to El Paso. See what Stoudenmire has to say.'

Fernandez and his *vaqueros* arrived in El Paso to find that the marshal had gone to New Mexico to execute a batch of warrants. It was evident that while the city council in El Paso were finding some of his character traits hard to contend with, other towns were still finding his services indispensable. His team of deputies kept the peace in El Paso while he was away but they were not the kind of men Fernandez felt he could approach. He decided that Stoudenmire had shown them the way and that now they must follow it again.

'We ride,' he said to Jose. 'Now.'

Felix Manning had ridden to the Hale ranch. He was told on arrival that Josh Hale had been arrested by the Texas Rangers and had been shot trying to escape. He was now dead. This was just

Two Dead in Three Seconds

what Felix Manning had known was going to happen and he was pleased it had come to pass. He was at the Hale ranch now to consolidate the Manning hold on it. Most of the herd dispersed by the Mexican raid on it not many days ago had been rounded up. The cattle stolen from across the border the night before had been added to it and the whole herd was being driven to the Southern Pacific railhead to be hauled to market in Dallas. By seven that evening it was planned that the cattle-trucks would be pulling out of El Paso.

Fernandez and his men were just about to ride out of El Paso when he was informed of what was happening.

'Where are the Rangers?' he asked his informant.

'At their camp at Ysleta,' the *vaquero* replied.

Fernandez pondered for a while. He was not happy about acting in Stoudenmire's absence but the way things were he didn't see that he had much choice.

'OK, my friend, thank you,' he said to his informant. Turning to Jose, he said, 'We will take the train, but we need more men.'

Pulling out a pocket-watch, he saw that it was

nearly four o'clock. They would have to ride hard. They were going to take the train half-way between El Paso and Ysleta. It would mean having to dynamite the track. But if the Rangers were keeping their noses out of things in Ysleta, he couldn't see that it should present any major difficulties. Just as before, he knew the element of surprise would be on their side.

There was a lot of whistling and yelping down at the cattle yards at the El Paso cattle depot. Things were not moving as fast as they should but the Manning drive boss was sure they'd get the cattle penned and loaded in time. No one was worried about Mexicans, and the train, when it pulled out of Union Station on time, was no better guarded than it might normally have been. Only thing was, among the passengers was a company of soldiers and their officers travelling home on leave from Fort Bliss to their families in towns dotted along the Southern Pacific line eastwards.

Fernandez and his men experienced no difficulty riding to where they planned to dynamite the track. There was a full moon and they knew the terrain better than anyone. Arriving at their

Two Dead in Three Seconds

destination, their explosives expert set to work.

'OK, Manuel, we have about twenty-five minutes before the train is due,' Fernandez said to him. 'The cattle-trucks will be at the end but we want to derail the engine.'

'Sí, sí, señor, don't worry.' Manuel, a veteran whose expertise in the years before had helped clear the way for the railroad company to lay their tracks in the area, said as he set to work.

He placed thirty sticks of dynamite in strategic places along a ten-foot length of the track and then joined them all with wire, which he then connected to a plunger fifty yards away from the track behind some boulders. As he checked his connections to the plunger and wound up the generator, the train could be heard coming.

'All right,' Fernandez said to Jose, 'keep the men well away from the track so they can't be seen as the train approaches. When the train has stopped take half the men to the rear and unload the cattle trucks. The rest of us will watch the train for trouble. If there is any trouble leave it to us to sort out. You get the cattle away.'

Then they all waited. The train was carrying a full payload and it was not coming fast. It was a warm night and most of the passengers were

Two Dead in Three Seconds

already beginning to nod off, the company of soldiers amongst them. Tension mounted amongst the Mexicans as they waited for the train to draw level with them. Fernandez, pleased that Stoudenmire had asked him to be his best man, wondered how he'd view what they were about to do.

As the train came into view, Manuel wound up the plunger and got ready to depress it. It was a long train with about twelve carriages. Half were passenger carriages and they lit up the track either side. As the train came on tension began to mount even higher among the Mexicans. Manuel watched and waited as the train came almost level with them, using all his experience to gauge the moment carefully. As the outline of the driver in his locomotive came into view he pushed down the plunger. The exploding dynamite lifted the locomotive a few inches into the air, derailing it as it came crashing down. For a moment there was a dead silence broken only by the hissing of stream as it escaped from the engine. Then slowly the shocked and startled people on the train began to stir.

The soldiers were in the last of the passenger carriages. Their carriage was still on the tracks

Two Dead in Three Seconds

and they had been no more than a little thrown about by the derailment of the locomotive and some of the front carriages.

'Be prepared for action, men,' one of their officers called out. 'This could be a hold-up.'

That it was so was suddenly confirmed to him by the sound of the *vaqueros* charging up to the cattle trucks and opening them, whistling and hollering as they tried to drive the cattle out.

'To your arms, men!' the officer ordered, 'and fire freely at anything out there that moves.'

The first barrage of shots took the *vaqueros* by surprise and a number of them fell. Fernandez and his contingent of *vaqueros* quickly grasped what was happening and sprang into action. There were over fifty of them and they let rip a storm of lead that thumped into the carriage carrying the soldiers, killing or wounding all those at the windows firing.

The *vaqueros* unloading the cattle had been thrown into confusion by the rifle fire levied at them and were wheeling about on their horses, firing into the soldiers' carriage.

'Get the cattle off the trucks,' Fernandez called out to them. 'Leave the rest to us.'

There was still fire coming from the soldiers'

carriage but considerably less of it and soon there was none. When it was obvious the firing had ceased Fernandez pulled up close to the carriage and looked in through the shattered windows. He had assumed that the men in the carriage must have been Texas Rangers somehow or other tipped off about their plans and was surprised to see the bodies of men dressed in army uniforms.

'Sweet Jesus!' he muttered away to himself, suddenly realizing that the situation had now become very serious. Just then Jose rode up to him. He looked into the carriage and then looked into the face of his leader.

'What now?' he asked, his expression grave.

'Come on,' Fernandez said to him, pulling his horse round and looking at the cattle being herded by his men. 'We must get these beeves across the border as quickly as possible.'

'What the hell!' the colonel in charge of the garrison at Fort Bliss exclaimed when told of what had happened. 'Outlaws hold up trains to rob them and their passengers of cash and valuables, but they don't hold them up to rustle cattle!'

'They were Mexicans, sir,' a lieutenant informed him.

Two Dead in Three Seconds

'Mexicans?'

'Yes, sir, from across the border. It seems some of their cattle were rustled and put on the train to be shipped to market and they decided to take them back.'

It was soon accepted that the Mexicans couldn't have known there'd be soldiers on board the train. Not knowing whether or not it was the job of the army or the civilian authorities to retaliate, the colonel decided to send a dispatch to the state capital before taking any action.

What had happened outraged the Manning brothers and they argued it could only have happened at the instigation of Stoudenmire.

'This time he's gonna pay!' James Manning declared at a meeting with some of the members of the city council and the mayor held in the mayor's office.

'Now let's not be hasty in blaming the marshal for this,' the mayor, who was no admirer of the Manning brothers, said. 'Why, he ain't even in Texas!'

'Why not?' asked Felix Manning. 'He led the Mexicans in the raid on the Hale ranch.'

'Yes,' agreed Mayor Schultz, 'but he gave us a

convincing explanation for that. However, he signed the peace treaty with you and promised nothing like it would ever happen again. No, I think the Mexican *vaqueros* acted alone.'

'I don't,' insisted James Manning, adding: 'I mean, he asked their leader to be best man at his wedding, after all.'

'What's at the root of all this,' one of the city councillors interjected, 'is the fact that someone is stealing cattle from the Mexicans and bringing them across the border. Stop that and there'll be no trouble here in El Paso with Mexicans.'

James and Felix Manning were quick to sense that what the councillor, one of the few in the city who were not in some way indebted to them, had said was pointed at them but the look on their faces would not have said so.

'It's the job of the Texas Rangers to find out who and so far they ain't come up with nothing,' James Manning remarked.

'That was precisely Marshal Stoudenmire's complaint,' the mayor said, eyeballing James Manning to drive home more fully the point he was trying to make.

'I know what that man has being trying to pin on my brothers and me in trying to ruin our good

Two Dead in Three Seconds

name in this city,' Manning, his voice full of anger and indignation, said, 'but he ain't gonna succeed. He's a no-good drunk and the sooner the city council realize it and get rid of him the better. But in the meantime, we've lost three hundred head of prime beef cattle and we'd like to know what's gonna be done about it.'

The mayor replied that the matter was being investigated. He added that Marshal Stoudenmire was expected back in town that day or the next and that it would fall to him to complete the investigation on behalf of the city. The Manning brothers left the meeting with ideas of their own about investigating what had happened but kept them firmly to themselves. Nevertheless, as the mayor left his office he and his councillors wore worried expressions on their faces.

Stoudenmire roared with laughter when, on his return to El Paso, he heard what had happened to the Manning brothers' consignment of beef.

Fernandez and his *vaqueros*, he thought, were quick on the uptake. Mayor Solomon Schultz could not be so sanguine about it.

'I don't see why you find the affair something

Two Dead in Three Seconds

to laugh about,' the mayor remarked to the marshal when the amused look seemed to linger on his face. 'After all, twenty or more soldiers were killed in the hold-up.'

'That I agree was most unfortunate, Mayor. But you can hardly blame the Mexicans for that,' was Stoudenmire's reply.

The mayor was at a loss to appreciate the logic behind the marshal's reply, but chose not to pursue the matter. Instead he said, 'I am expecting you to get to the bottom of the affair and bring someone to book over it.'

'What about the army?' Stoudenmire asked.

'They're leaving it to the civil authorities, which means you and the Texas Rangers. You are expected to work with them.'

Stoudenmire's expression suddenly became very serious. 'Mayor,' he said, 'you know as well as I do that the Manning brothers have been stealing Mexican cattle. The Texas Rangers knew it and did nothing about it, because they were bribed not to. Now you're saying they're gonna go in pursuit of the Mexicans whose only intention was to take back what was theirs. And you expect me to join in? Do you know what that will do to the law and order we've established here in El Paso?'

Two Dead in Three Seconds

'Soldiers, American citizens, were killed, Marshal.'

'And a lot more American citizens are gonna die if you start a border war with the Mexicans, Mayor. Which is what you will be doing if the Texas Rangers are sent in.'

The mayor thought for a while and then, throwing his hands up in the air, said, 'Well, it's out of my hands now, Marshal. Someone has to be seen to pay and that's really all there is to it.'

Leaving the mayor's office Stoudenmire decided he had to see Fernandez. He was due to be married in less than a week and Fernandez was going to be his best man. This he saw was likely to give rise to a few problems. As he walked down the boardwalk in the direction of the Silver Dollar Hotel he came face to face with James Manning. Neither man gave ground to the other and they came to a halt almost face to face.

'What d'you think of your Mexican friends now?' James Manning spat out at him after a second's penetrating look into Stoudenmire's eyes.

'Clever little bastards, I'd say, wouldn't you?' replied Stoudenmire.

'That's not what the Texas Rangers think, which would, I'd say, make them *dead* clever little bastards,' Manning replied.

Stoudenmire said nothing, but instead gave Manning a menacing look. Manning was unruffled. He was confident that soon the marshal would pay for all the irritations he'd caused them since coming to town and he was prepared to climb down over this one and let the marshal pass by.

'Whatever, we'll see,' he said in the smoothest possible tones to Stoudenmire, while stepping aside to allow him to pass by.

Stoudenmire realized he was up to something, but could only guess what.

ELEVEN

Fernandez and his *vaqueros* had been lying low in a village in the mountains south-east of El Paso. Though the Texas Rangers had so far come up with nothing in their search for him, Stoudenmire had no problem finding Fernandez. The Mexicans on the border saw him as a friend and they had led him straight to him.

'Looks like you've lost your best man,' were Fernandez's first words to Stoudenmire.

'As before, you only took back what was yours,' he replied.

It wasn't so much a love of Mexicans, or even a sense of natural justice that made Stoudenmire look at things the way he did. It was the killing of his friend Doc Cummings that had pushed him over the edge.

Two Dead in Three Seconds

'Not the Mannings, nor anyone else, are gonna ruin my wedding plans,' he said to Fernandez. 'And those plans involve you handing me the rings. It's what me and Belle want.'

'You're some kind of strange gringo,' Fernandez replied.

Stoudenmire simply smiled. Then he and Fernandez got down to drinking and making some plans. By dawn they were both so drunk it took the rest of the day for them to sleep it off before Stoudenmire was fit enough to get on his horse for the ride back to Texas. As Stoudenmire crossed the border, he was confronted by a company of Texas Rangers. The captain in charge knew exactly, as indeed did all of them, what Stoudenmire must have been doing across the border.

'You gonna tell us where they are?' he asked.

Stoudenmire, who was simply going to ride around the Rangers without saying a word, reined in his mount. He studied the captain for a moment and then said, 'You gonna kiss my ass?'

Sitting up in his saddle and casting am impatient look around him, the captain replied, 'Marshal, I can arrest you now and take you in for a multitude of charges and most of the citizens of El Paso would thank me for it.'

'Don't you mean the Manning brothers?' remarked Stoudenmire.

He still had a bit of a hangover and a headache and was beginning to feel his temper fray.

'What's the Manning brothers got to do with this?' asked the captain, who had a tough enough exterior not to let anything show.

'Ain't they been supplementing your wages, Captain?'

'Marshal, I resent what you're saying,' the captain replied firmly. 'Now are you gonna tell me where Fernandez and his men are hiding out or am I gonna arrest you?'

Dusk was falling and the air was beginning to fill with the sound of insects. They were on the ridge of a steep hill and as the captain and Stoudenmire sat squarely in their saddles eyeballing one another a cold breeze began to blow up. It played with the brims of their Stetsons and added to a sense felt by all concerned that a moment of truth had come into the proceedings.

As well as their leader, there were ten Rangers. Stoudenmire knew that if he went for his gun his chances would not be very good. The only thing that made him worry about that was the thought of Belle. She'd been a woman of wild ways, though not as wild as people would have it, and he'd always admired her for it. When he'd come to El Paso he hadn't reckoned on meeting her there and finding she'd now become the settling down kind. But he had found her and they'd developed a fondness for one another. Fondness for a woman was a new thing to him but he guessed that it was not so much that Belle was a woman but that she was Belle. Whatever was behind it, he liked being attached to her. Looking at the captain now, he thought he wasn't going to let any two-bit, thirty-dollar-a-month son of a bitch ruin it for him.

What he would have done next will have to remain a mystery, because suddenly, as if from nowhere, a group of about a hundred Mexicans began to encircle them. Somehow, Stoudenmire was not surprised, but the Texas Rangers were.

'What the. . . ?' their captain exclaimed looking about him.

'You were looking for them, now you've found them,' Stoudenmire said to him, smirking.

He reined his horse around to look for Fernandez, who, in fact, was not there. He was

Two Dead in Three Seconds

still in the village nursing a sore head. But Jose was there.

'We were told there was gonna be a raid on our cattle tonight, Marshal,' he said to Stoudenmire. 'You think these are the people who were gonna carry it out?'

'No, but I don't suppose they'd have done very much to stop it.'

'Now look here, Stoudenmire,' the captain suddenly declared in angry tones.

'No,' interrupted the marshal, 'you look here. These men here are farmers turned into bandits because of your corruption. If there's twenty or more dead US soldiers, it's your fault, not theirs, and you're gonna have to pay for it.'

The captain and his Rangers looked decidedly uncomfortable. Now it was their turn to ponder the implications of a shoot-out.

'Do what you want with them,' Stoudenmire said, looking at Jose.

One of the Texas Rangers made a movement and suddenly the guns of one hundred and more Mexicans were pointed at all of them and cocked.

'Looks like I ain't the one that's gonna be arrested today,' Stoudenmire remarked, looking at the captain. 'Thank you, *compadre*,' he turned and said to Jose. 'As I said, do what you like with them.'

'*Sí*, Marshal,' Jose replied.

'Maybe,' Stoudenmire added, as he began to leave, 'they'll do what they get paid by the good state of Texas to do, and help stop your cattle being rustled tonight.'

As he began to ride away he made a point of going through the middle of the Rangers. Looking the captain squarely in the eyes he smiled sardonically and said, 'Ain't life sometimes just a bitch?'

'You'll pay for this,' the captain muttered, full of anger and indignation, which only caused Stoudenmire's smile to spread even wider.

TWELVE

Stoudenmire rode into El Paso around eleven the next morning. As he entered El Paso Street he was seen by James Manning who was on his way to the Coliseum Saloon. As he passed by, Stoudenmire tipped his hat. The sight of the marshal riding into town on his own, a free man, came as something of a surprise to Manning. Stoudenmire could see this in his face and it confirmed what he'd already assumed.

'Son of a bitch!' James Manning exclaimed to his brother Felix as he stormed up to the bar in the Coliseum and threw his Stetson down on the counter. 'I just saw Stoudenmire riding down El Paso Street free as a coyote.'

'How'd he manage that?' Felix asked.

Two Dead in Three Seconds

'Montgomery and his Rangers must have missed him.'

A little later on in the morning they heard that their raid on the Mexican herds the evening before had been expected and that most of their men had been killed.

'Something's got to be done about that Stoudenmire and soon,' stormed James Manning, 'before our whole cattle operation collapses. We got orders to complete and deliveries to make.'

The two brothers thought for a moment and then Felix said, 'He's getting married Saturday, ain't he?'

'Yeah,' replied James.

'Well, we'll get him then.'

James studied his brother for a moment and then asked, 'How?'

'We'll have men on the roofs of the buildings opposite the church and when he comes out we'll have him.'

'And Belle? What if she gets hit?'

'What if she does?' his brother sneered. 'George'd be alive now if it wasn't for her two-timing him. Whatever she gets she deserves.'

'And the rest of the town? Most of them's bound to be there.'

Two Dead in Three Seconds

Felix thought for a moment and then replied, 'I'm sick of this town and its fawning at the feet of Dallas Stoudenmire. It's time it was taught a lesson. This was our town before that drunken bum came riding in and we'll show Schultz and the rest of the city council that it's gonna be ours again.'

Just as he was finishing what he was saying one of their cowboys came riding up to the boardwalk, jumped off his horse and hurried into the saloon.

'Mexicans got the whole company of Texas Rangers,' he informed the two brothers, who looked anxiously from one to the other as the man spoke.

'You sure?' James asked, instructing the barkeep with gestures made by his right hand to give the man a drink.

'Sure as I know anything. The marshal crossed the border and was confronted by the Rangers and they in turn was surrounded by a big bunch of Mexicans. Stoudenmire was freed and the Rangers taken to the Mexicans' hideout in the hills.'

The Manning brothers were quiet for a moment, taking in the implications of what they'd just heard. Then Felix spoke.

'That's it, Jim. We gotta do what I said, before things go too far.'

Word of what had happened to the Texas Rangers soon spread around El Paso. One of the first to hear of it was Mayor Schultz. Without waiting for Stoudenmire to make a call on him, he went straight round to the Silver Dollar Hotel, where he'd been told the marshal was. It was not yet lunchtime. When he arrived there Stoudenmire was upstairs in one of Belle's room luxuriating in a hot, soapy, hip-bath. Belle had just finished scrubbing his back and had handed him a lighted cheroot, when one of her girls knocked on the door to tell her Mayor Schultz was downstairs asking for the marshal.

'I didn't think it'd be long before he'd want to see me,' Stoudenmire said to Belle. 'Give the man a drink and tell him I'll be down presently.'

Mayor Schultz was not the drinking kind and he declined Belle's offer. Mayor Schultz in fact did not like finding himself at all in an establishment such as Belle Star's, and it showed clearly in his uncomfortable demeanour. Would his wife or anyone else believe that he'd gone in there simply on business?

Figuring this, Belle said to him, 'Mayor, would you rather we went somewhere more private? I mean to say less public.'

Belle's obvious charms, well honed now to fit her current occupation, never failed to work their magic and the mayor found himself warming to her.

'I don't believe,' he found himself saying, 'that I have had the opportunity to congratulate you on your forthcoming wedding to the marshal, ma'am.'

'Why, thank you,' Belle replied courteously. 'I do hope you and your good wife will do Dallas and me the honour of being our guests. Both at the church and here afterwards for the wedding breakfast.'

'Well, that's mighty kind of you, ma'am. I shall pass on your kind invitation to Mrs Schultz and I am sure she and I will be most happy to accept.'

Belle's girls and members of the drinking public sitting around were amused by this exchange between Belle and the mayor. For them the wedding was going to be an excuse for an almighty shindig and the thought of the dignitaries being there was highly interesting to say the least.

'And, of course, that invitation is extended to all the city councillors and their wives,' Belle added.

Before the mayor could reply Stoudenmire appeared at the top of the stairs leading from the first floor of the hotel down to the bar. He didn't immediately begin to descend the stairs, but instead stood on the landing, straightening his clean clothes and arranging his guns to sit comfortably in his pockets. He was a giant of a man with the formidable look of the assured gunfighter who'd won every shoot-out he'd ever been in.

'Mayor Shultz,' he said at last, coming down the stairs. 'I am sorry I had to keep you waiting.'

They finished exchanging pleasantries and then got down to why the mayor was there.

'I might, if I may, ma'am,' Schultz said, turning to Belle, 'take you up on your offer of somewhere more private to speak.'

'Of course,' Belle replied, leading the two men to her office, which was situated behind the bar, and instructing a clerk who was working there to leave them alone.

'Thank you, ma'am,' the mayor said to Belle and the office door was closed upon them. Then

Two Dead in Three Seconds

to Stoudenmire he said, 'To get straight to the point, Marshal, news has come to me of the Rangers being taken prisoner by Mexicans and your involvement in the affair. Can you explain yourself?'

What the mayor said, to Stoudenmire came to him as no surprise and he had his answer ready.

'I told you before, Mayor, that they were in the pay of the Manning brothers and now they have paid the price for it.'

'But what was your involvement and how come the Mexicans let you go?' Schultz asked him.

'I had been across the border to talk to Fernandez and his men to find out exactly what happened on the night the soldiers were killed. I was on my way back to El Paso when the Rangers tried to arrest me. The Mexicans coming along when they did prevented the situation ending in more bloodshed.'

'On what grounds were the Rangers trying to arrest you?' the mayor asked.

'I assumed on the orders of the Manning brothers.'

'Come, come, Marshal. You have signed a peace treaty with James and Felix Manning.'

Stoudenmire smiled cynically. 'You don't get it,

do you, Mayor? That treaty simply played into the hands of those no-good sons of bitches. You pinned a badge on me to clean up this town, which I have to a large degree done, wouldn't you agree?'

'I will not deny that you and your deputies have brought a considerable degree of law and order to the streets of our city—'

'And there would have been an awful lot more of it but for the antics of the Manning brothers. I should arrest them on charges of cattle-rustling but it's obvious I wouldn't get them to stick. The Mexicans know this, which is why they have taken the law into their own hands. All I have been trying to do is stop a major border incident happening. A job I've had to take it upon myself to do simply because the Rangers were being paid not to do it by the Mannings. And now a company of soldiers has paid the price for their corruption. This town is half Mexican, Mayor. There could never be peace in it so long as they felt justice was being denied them. You'll remember what happened at the inquest into the death of the *vaqueros*? If I hadn't been there to stop it, the whole city would have erupted into war.'

Two Dead in Three Seconds

The mayor could not avoid the truth of what was being said to him. He thought for a moment and then asked Stoudenmire, 'Can you bring me any proof that the Mannings have been stealing Mexican cattle and bringing it across the border?'

The marshal again responded with a cynical laugh. 'Proof that would stand up in court, when they own half the citizens of any note?'

'So what's to be done?'

'Don't ask me. Ask the Texas Rangers. My job is to keep law and order on the streets of El Paso, and that is what I aim to do. One of these days the Mannings will go too far and when they do I'll be waiting for them.'

'And in the meantime?'

'I told you, it's a problem for the Rangers, not us. I sent a telegram to General King in Austin telling him of what was happening and it got me nowhere. Perhaps he'll sit up and take notice now.'

The mayor looked a very worried man. 'And this wedding of yours to Miss Starr, you intend to go ahead with it?' he asked.

'I don't see any reason not to,' the marshal replied.

Two Dead in Three Seconds

'With Fernandez as your best man?'

Stoudenmire thought for a moment and then replied.

'I'd have asked Doc Cummings, but since he was murdered, I couldn't. Fernandez is a friend of mine. The Mexicans know that as long as they stick to the law they have nothing to fear from me in this town. Fernandez is their leader. It might help to improve relations.'

'But he's wanted for murder. If he sets a foot on American soil either the Rangers or the army will have him.'

'Well, yes, I do agree, Mayor, that does present something of a problem.'

From his tone of voice, though, the mayor could see it was not a problem that unduly worried the marshal. He became even more concerned for the welfare of the peaceable citizens of El Paso, whom it was his job to represent.

'Well,' he said, sighing, 'you're the law in this city, Marshal, and as it says in the *Lone Star*, the city council must either back you or sack you. I can only hope that you know what you're doing.'

It was obvious to Stoudenmire that the mayor felt he had no choice but to back him.

Two Dead in Three Seconds

'Let me do my job, Mayor,' he said reassuringly, 'and I think you'll see I do.'

THIRTEEN

A political situation had developed. A large number of American soldiers had been killed and now a company of Texas Rangers had been taken captive – by a bunch of Mexicans; this was asking for trouble and the powers that be in the state capital, Austin, had decided Mexico was going to get it.

Everyone in El Paso, Stoudenmire included, was aware of the sudden flurry of activity in Fort Bliss. The army had begun to send out patrols and Texas Ranger reinforcements began to arrive. What galvanized Stoudenmire into taking some sort of action was the fact that his wedding-day was fast approaching. Added to this was the fact that he knew that unless he did something a lot of innocent Mexicans on the border were going

Two Dead in Three Seconds

to suffer. He decided he had to send word to Fernandez that he had to release the Texas Rangers. It was the only thing that would take the heat out of the situation. He went to see whom he knew in El Paso who would get a message through. The Manning brothers had watched his every move closely since he'd arrived back in El Paso. He was unaware of this but had he known he wouldn't have cared. He was almost willing them into a showdown while instinctively knowing that one was not going to come yet.

Fernandez had the Texas Rangers imprisoned in an old mission about twenty miles inside the border.

'OK,' he said when he received word from Stoudenmire. 'Tell him I will release the Rangers at dawn tomorrow morning. They'll have a long walk. They'll get hot and thirsty but they will arrive back on the American side of the border unharmed.'

At first light the next day the Rangers were told they were free to go.

'What about our horses?' Captain Montgomery asked. Their horses had been taken from them when they had arrived at the old mission.

'We will keep them,' Jose said. 'For our trouble. Safe passage across the border is guaranteed but

Two Dead in Three Seconds

don't cause any trouble on the way. And don't come back. We cannot promise to be so – what shall I say? – easy on you next time.'

Montgomery looked at his men in disbelief. It had to be a trick.

'We will not leave without our horses,' he suddenly declared.

'Please yourself,' Jose replied. 'But you are no longer our prisoners.'

Turning away from the Rangers, Jose barked a few orders at his men and within a few minutes he and they had ridden away. The old mission, which was normally uninhabited, was suddenly abandoned again. Only the Rangers remained, looking baffled.

Word soon reached Stoudenmire that the Rangers were free. Immediately after breakfast he went to the mayor's office and informed Schultz of the fact and where they were likely to be found.

'You sure?' the mayor asked him.

'Go and inform them at Fort Bliss and they can go see,' Stoudenmire replied casually. 'I told you Fernandez does not want trouble. Just for their cattle to be left alone.'

The mayor quickly pulled on his jacket. 'You're

a strange man, Marshal,' he said to Stoudenmire.

'Just doing my job,' was all the marshal said in reply.

When James and Felix Manning heard what had happened they felt Stoudenmire had somehow or other got one over them. They'd been putting pressure on the people with whom they had influence to do something about the marshal, wanting them to impress upon the army and the Rangers that everything that had happened was entirely down to Stoudenmire's collusion with those they called the Mexican bandits. And now it was being made to look as if he had single-handedly taken the heat out of what had promised to develop into a major border incident between the United States and Mexico.

'God damn it, Jim!' exclaimed Felix. 'We gotta do something about that man.'

'When's he fixing to wed that harlot of his?' Jim asked.

'Saturday.'

'That's three days.'

'Yeah,' grinned Felix, knowing the wedding present he and his brother had planned to give to Stoudenmire.

Two Dead in Three Seconds

*

Before the prize of the Texas Rangers had fallen into their hands Stoudenmire and Fernandez had planned some distractions for the citizens of El Paso. Fernandez now began to put them into action. Over the next few days it appeared as if the Mexican part of the city had decided Stoudenmire's wedding to Belle Starr was an excuse for non-stop revelry. People from the surrounding villages flocked into the city for what became a three-day festival of drinking, music-making and dancing. The American citizens of El Paso could only look on in dismay.

'That man has got to be brought to book, Mayor. He has made a laughing-stock of the Texas Rangers and no one, but *no one*, gets away with doing that.'

It was Captain Montgomery.

'A laughing-stock, you may have been made, Captain, but if the army's intelligence is correct, you have the marshal to thank for your lives,' Mayor Schultz replied pointedly.

'We would not have been taken prisoner in the first place were it not for Stoudenmire cosying up to these damned Mexicans. General King demands he be arrested on charges of being implicated in the murder of the soldiers on the train Fernandez and his gang held up. Now are you going to contradict an order from the authorities in Austin or is the army going to be forced to declare martial law in this city?'

'In case you haven't noticed, Captain, practically all of Mexico is in town celebrating the forthcoming marriage of Marshal Stoudenmire to Miss Belle Starr. What do you think will happen if I arrest him now?'

'That, if I might say so, Mayor, is your problem, not mine.'

'Well, I think it could become your problem, if they decided to try and bust him out of jail. Added to which is the accusation made against you that you have been taking bribes from the Mannings to turn a blind eye to the rustling of Mexican cattle.'

'And I have told you that that is a damn lie.'

'Yeah, well, Captain, you can see the dilemma I am left in. Now I have told you that I have sent a telegram to General King spelling out the situation we find ourselves in here. He has wired back that he is sending down a team of special investigators to try and get to the bottom of the problems we are faced with. I am told they will arrive the day after the marshal's wedding. I think it would be prudent to leave matters as they are until then. The army agrees with me and I think that is where matters must rest for the moment.'

Captain Montgomery could see that he was getting nowhere with the mayor and decided he was wasting his time continuing the argument. The last thing he wanted was an official inquiry poking its nose into things. He took his leave of the mayor, intending right away to arrange a clandestine meeting with the Mannings before the day was out.

FOURTEEN

'Why, Belle, you look just beautiful!' declared Margaret on seeing Belle dressed in her wedding-gown for the final fitting on the night before the wedding.

'Not bad, I suppose,' Belle replied, eyeing herself in a long mirror while a seamstress put the finishing touches to her dress. 'Though I can't help but feel it's a bit more ladylike than I really like.'

Margaret was standing behind her and Belle could see her reflection in the mirror. She couldn't help but notice the look of sadness that suddenly spread across her face. Turning to face her and ignoring the seamstress who was adding a few stitches to the hem of her dress, she said, 'Why, Margaret, what is it?'

Two Dead in Three Seconds

'Oh nothing,' Belle's future sister-in-law replied, tears beginning to well up in her eyes.

Belle looked at her for a moment and then tenderly said, 'I know what it is, honey. It's Doc, isn't it?'

At the mention of her dead husband's name Margaret's tears began to flow.

'I know, honey, I know,' Belle said in comforting tones. 'We're all gonna feel it bad tomorrow knowing he ain't there. And Dallas will feel it as much as you.'

'Belle, before I met you I heard terrible stories about you, but you've been so kind to me I wouldn't want your big day spoilt for anything. And nor would Samuel have.'

As strong a woman as she was, Belle felt a lump in her throat at the kind thing Margaret had said to her. She even felt tears well in her own eyes. Not wanting to let them show, she turned away from Margaret to let the seamstress carry on with her work.

'One day those Mannings will pay. Dallas will see to that,' she said. 'And one day, Margaret, you will find happiness again. Doc would have wanted it. Of that, I am sure.'

Margaret Cummings sorrow ran too deep for

Two Dead in Three Seconds

Belle's words to have brought her any real comfort and she left Belle's bedroom to go to her own above the Globe Restaurant, there to cry herself to sleep. While she did so, her brother revelled and drank the last night of his bachelor life away with his friends in the Mexican part of town.

Dawn broke. Captain Montgomery's clandestine meeting with the Manning brothers had given him the comfort he was looking for and he was happy that by the end of the day Stoudenmire would be history. Dressed as civilians, he and a handful of his men took up their positions on the roofs of the buildings opposite the Baptist church before many of the citizens of El Paso began to stir. They were joined there by some of the Manning brothers' men. Together they lay low, well out of sight of people going about their business in the streets below.

Shortly after nine some of Belle's girls, directed by Margaret, arrived with arms full of flowers to decorate the church, and bunting to decorate the boardwalk outside it. Belle was in her bath in which the water had been scented. Her hairdresser was standing by. She and all the women

Two Dead in Three Seconds

were full of excitement, knowing the big day had at last arrived. The wedding was to take place at eleven.

Stoudenmire himself did not surface until gone nine. He was in Rosa's Cantina where he had collapsed in a drunken stupor in the wee small hours of the morning. Along with him were half a dozen or more *vaqueros*, amongst whom were Jose and Fernandez.

'What time is it?' he asked out loud, as he pulled himself into a sitting-up position and rubbed his eyes.

'Late enough,' replied Feleena, a serving girl who was clearing up the mess left from the night before.

As she spoke Rosa came into the room.

'Marshal!' she exclaimed in summary tones, 'today is the day when you will make one lady very happy.'

'Just give me some coffee, Rosa,' Stoudenmire replied, his mouth dry and his voice husky.

'Of course. I bring it right away. How about a Yankee breakfast of ham and eggs?'

Stoudenmire simply nodded in reply, running his hands through his hair and stretching.

At the sound of voices the others began to wake

Two Dead in Three Seconds

up and to get to their feet. Before long they were all drinking coffee and lighting up their first makings of the day. Very few words were spoken as they tried to get their heads together to greet the day. Seeing that it was getting near ten o'clock Stoudenmire realized that he had to get to his office where his wedding-suit was hanging and where he planned to get cleaned up in time to meet his bride at the altar in the church.

'OK, Fernandez, you know what to do,' he said.

'Are you sure you want to go through with this, Marshal?' Fernandez asked. 'I will understand if you want someone else to be your best man.'

Waving aside Francisco's concerns, Stoudenmire reminded him that he knew what to do and then left. He soon reached El Paso Street and began to walk down it. One of the first people he saw was James Manning, who was sitting on a hitching rail on the opposite side of the street outside the Coliseum Saloon nonchalantly smoking a cigarillo. Stoudenmire couldn't help but look over to him and their eyes met. Manning took a long drag on his cigarillo and blew the smoke out slowly. Nothing in his gaze told the marshal what he had in store for him later in the morning.

Stoudenmire's thoughts filled with memories

of Doc Cummings, as they always did when he caught sight of either of the brothers. The only comfort he took was from the thought that he was marrying the girl they had all assumed belonged to George, the brother Doc had put beneath the ground. But it was little comfort in the face of the great loss he felt over the death of Cummings.

Neither man attempted to face the other down. Stoudenmire had kept walking and it wasn't long before James Manning was out of his line of vision. Manning watched him go and then, getting up from the rail, flicked his half-smoked cigarillo into the street and stepped into the saloon.

'Morning, Marshal,' Deputy Marshal Irvine Jones greeted Stoudenmire as he stepped into his office. 'It sure is going to be a fine day for a wedding.'

Stoudenmire liked Jones. He was a competent man who played his part in keeping law and order in the city in a brave way.

'Guess I'd agree with you, Jones, if I didn't have such a doggone head.'

'I ain't commenting on that,' Jones, who was a teetotaller, smiled. 'I don't reckon I got a right to.'

Two Dead in Three Seconds

'Gimme some coffee,' was all Stoudenmire said in reply.

'Sure thing, Marshal,' Jones said, taking a tin mug and filling it with coffee from a pot on a stove in a corner of the office. 'Water's ready for you to wash and shave. Your suit's hanging up, there's a clean shirt and your boots have been polished. Reckon you've just about got time to get ready.'

Taking the mug of coffee from Jones's hand, Stoudenmire thanked him. 'Don't know what I'd do without you,' he added.

Kind words indeed, Jones thought, smiling to himself, coming from a man such as he. 'Seen Margaret and the girls making the church and boardwalk look mighty pretty,' he remarked.

Stoudenmire gave nothing more than a grunt, in reply, as he downed his coffee, wondering if he wouldn't do better simply to call on the barber. Normally he liked to shave himself but today he reckoned he didn't have a steady enough hand. He didn't want to greet Belle with blood on his face.

While the marshal readied himself for his big day, the streets around the church began slowly to fill with people. A big showing of dignitaries was expected and the ordinary people of El Paso didn't want to miss out on seeing them. Added to which, of course, the womenfolk all wanted to see Belle in her wedding dress. Soon there were a hundred or more people gathered. As they waited chatting expectantly amongst themselves the festive sounds of a mariachi band began to fill the air as a huge parade of Mexicans began to process down El Paso Street. This was a side of Mexican life the American citizens of the city couldn't help but warm to. The procession came level with the Silver Dollar Hotel in time to coincide with Belle climbing into a wedding buggy. As it pulled away it fell in line behind her, the band playing and the people singing a Mexican folk song that announced the coming of the bride.

Ahead of them, to the cheers of the people, Stoudenmire stepped into the church. No dignitaries had shown up, but this had as yet gone unnoticed by the crowd as it revelled in the joyous arrival of the bride. Stoudenmire noticed but was not surprised. Politics, he sneered to himself. Where were the sentiments of 'back him or sack him' now? Still, he thought, striding down to the altar, taking in the beautiful decorations and returning the smiles of the people greeting

Two Dead in Three Seconds

him from the pews, he wasn't going to let them spoil Belle's big day.

Seconds after he took up his position in front of the altar the congregation gasped as he was joined by a man entering from a side door. It was Fernandez. No other Mexican would dare enter the church, he was the only one.

'Sorry it ain't a Catholic church,' Stoudenmire joked as he took him by the hand.

'No problem, Marshal. God will forgive me,' Fernandez replied, beaming and looking magnificent in his traditional Mexican best.

Soon all eyes were averted from Fernandez as the church organist struck up the tune that traditionally accompanies the bride's entrance into the church. A prettier picture could not have greeted their eyes, many of which, those belonging to the women, misted over. Stoudenmire was simply overwhelmed and went through the ceremony as if on a cloud. So tough a man and feisty a lady became, for the magical duration, the perfect prince and princess.

The ceremony over, the congregation couldn't help but clap as the bridal march carried the newly weds down the aisle and out of the door of the church to the steps. Watching and waiting on

Two Dead in Three Seconds

the roofs opposite, James and Felix Manning and their men, along with Captain Montgomery and his Rangers, cocked their weapons and lined up their sights.

The first shot missed its target. It was fired by Felix Manning and was aimed at Stoudenmire's smiling face. But it missed as the marshal turned and bent to kiss his bride. Though few heard its crack above the cheering of the crowd and the sound of the *mariachi* band playing, all saw it slap into the door frame and send splinters flying. As more shots rang out panic gripped the crowd and people began to flee in all directions.

Stoudenmire's first reaction had been to push Belle and his sister Margaret, who had been Belle's matron of honour, back into the safety of the church. Then he pulled the guns he never went anywhere without from his pockets. Guns and rifles also appeared in the hands of many of the Mexican men who had paraded down El Paso Street. These were the *vaqueros*. They dived for cover behind anything available and let loose a storm of lead at the men shooting from the rooftops.

As Captain Montgomery fell dead at their side, the Manning brothers were completely taken by

Two Dead in Three Seconds

surprise. Cursing his brother for missing his target, James Manning fixed his sights on Stoudenmire, but none of his shots struck home. He looked on in horror as people in the crowd fell to the ground wounded and dying. Stoudenmire had taken cover behind the church doors, firing non-stop up at the rooftops. Fernandez had dived behind a water-trough in front of the church and was picking off men on the roof with at least every other shot he fired.

'Dallas,' Belle called to her husband, 'give me a gun.'

Margaret was on the floor of the church along with the congregation.

'No, Belle, stay where you are,' Stoudenmire replied.

Taking stock of the situation, he knew one or both of the Manning brothers had to be on the roof opposite firing at them. Believing that Fernandez and his men would keep them at bay, he decided he had to get up on the roof and get behind them. As he began to weave a way through the congregation to the side door of the church, Belle called out to him again that she wanted a gun.

'No, Belle,' he called over his shoulder, 'just

stay here and take care of Margaret.'

Once out of the church and in a side-street he made his way to where, unnoticed by anyone, he could cross El Paso Street and get behind the buildings the firing was coming from. By now the army had become alerted to the slaughter that was taking place in the city and a company of soldiers was grabbing its weapons and getting ready to intervene.

Both James and Felix Manning had so far survived the gun-battle. Ducking down behind cover, James pulled up close to his brother and said, 'Felix, we gotta get away.'

'What do you mean?' Felix asked him.

'Maybe no one's seen us yet. If we get away they'll think it was Montgomery.'

'But what about them?' Felix asked, pointing at the men who were still alive and shooting down into the street. There were only about six of them.

'This,' James replied, turning his gun on them and firing.

Quick to realize why he was doing it, Felix also turned his gun on the men and with his brother finished them off.

'Come on,' James said, getting to his feet. He hurried towards a door that would take them to

Two Dead in Three Seconds

the stairs that led down to the street behind the building they'd been shooting from.

Hurrying, they were half-way down the stairs when they came up against Stoudenmire. Firing first, he killed James Manning who was leading his brother. The force of the bullet was not strong enough to stop him in his tracks and he fell on top of Stoudenmire, pinning him down.

'Now I've got you,' Felix spat as he stood over the marshal pointing a gun at his head.

As he cocked the gun and began to close his finger on the trigger a shot rang out and he fell backward, wounded in the chest. Succeeding at last in getting out from under the corpse of James Manning and on to his feet, Stoudenmire looked to see where the shot had come from.

'Belle!' he gasped, as he looked in disbelief at who it was that had fired it.

Then he heard Felix Manning begin to stir. Turning around, he saw that he was weakly levelling a gun at him. As he raised his own and pulled back the hammer, he said, 'The bullet that's gonna kill me ain't been made yet.' So saying he shot him between the eyes.

*

Two Dead in Three Seconds

The sight that greeted Stoudenmire when he stepped back into El Paso Street with Belle was one of utter carnage. The army had arrived, as had the mayor and members of the city council. While Belle began to help with the victims and their relatives, Stoudenmire sought out Fernandez. He did not, though, get far.

'Marshal,' the angry voice of the mayor called out to him, 'what in God's name happened here?'

Stoudenmire turned to face him and some of his councillors. 'You ask me?' he said, looking into all their faces with a penetrating, accusing stare. 'You ask me?'

'You and your damned feud with the Manning brothers!' exclaimed a distraught member of the city council.

'Feud? What feud?' he spat out at them between gritted teeth. 'The only "feud", as you call it, between myself and the Mannings was they wanted to carry on breaking the law and it was my job to make sure they obeyed it. I told this city weeks ago that they had the Rangers in their pockets but you wouldn't listen. Now you've had to pay the price.'

Neither the mayor nor the city council could counter what he was saying. They looked as sick

Two Dead in Three Seconds

as pigs and more worried than Job. Heads were going to have to roll for this and they knew the editor of the El Paso *Lone Star* was going to demand it be theirs.

'If you hadn't got so friendly with the Mexicans . . .' another town councillor began.

'If it hadn't been for Fernandez and his men more people would have died and the Manning brothers would still be alive,' Stoudenmire interrupted him. As he did so he suddenly became aware of what was going on further up El Paso Street. The army was rounding up the Mexicans and disarming them. Turning on the mayor, he said to him,

'Schultz, you're gonna come with me and tell the army to free those men or you're gonna have another bloodbath on your hands.'

The mayor tried to raise an objection but Stoudenmire, he knew, was going to have none of it.

'You're forgetting, Marshal,' he said as he fell in beside him, 'that Fernandez and his men killed a company of American soldiers.'

'I ain't forgetting nothing,' Stoudenmire replied firmly.

They quickly reached the army and Stoudenmire

demanded to know what was going on. As he did so he looked amongst the Mexicans they'd rounded up for the face of Fernandez but could not see it. Smiling inwardly, he thought, no, he wouldn't have hung around to wait for this. Nor would he have allowed his men to.

'What are you doing?' he asked the officer in charge.

'Arresting these here Mexicans on suspicion of holding up the train and killing our boys,' the officer, a young lieutenant, replied.

'Well, I think you'll find you got the wrong Mexicans.'

'What?' he replied, looking from Stoudenmire to the group of about twenty Mexicans his men were guarding.

'Do they look like fearless *bandidos* to you?' Stoudenmire asked him, pointing at what was patently a group of ordinary-looking townspeople, Mexican or otherwise.

'I tried to tell him, Marshal,' called a man whom Stoudenmire knew to be a barber in the Mexican part of town, 'but he wouldn't listen.'

'These are not the men you are looking for, Lieutenant, and I suggest you release them,' Stoudenmire said.

Two Dead in Three Seconds

'But I have my orders—' the lieutenant began to say.

'Just let them go,' the mayor interjected wearily. 'Just let them go.'

'I will have to talk to my commanding officer first.'

At this point Stoudenmire lost his temper. 'Lieutenant, I run this town, not the army. You've seen what happened here this morning to men who thought they and not I ran it. Now, are you gonna release these good people or am I gonna have to force you to do it?'

The lieutenant hesitated for a moment, looking from the marshal to the mayor, to the group of Mexicans and then back to the marshal.

'All right,' he said. 'But be it on your shoulders.'

Ain't it been all along and won't it always be? Stoudenmire muttered to himself in reply.

As the soldiers put down their guns and let the Mexicans go, the barber called out a thank you, adding, 'You're a good man, Marshal.'

But they were sentiments only the Mexicans of El Paso were prepared to concede were true. Nevertheless all the citizens were glad that Stoudenmire stayed on as marshal. Whatever else, he made them feel safe. He stayed on in the

Two Dead in Three Seconds

short term to make sure Fernandez and his men were cleared of deliberately shooting the soldiers. In the long term, he stayed on because the city council begged him to, knowing that whether they liked it or not, the peace of the West could only be kept by the likes of men whose fearlessness was rooted in mankind's God-given desire to not let evil win.